**"Thank You."**

Megan leaned to kiss his cheek in a heartfelt thank you just as he turned to answer.

Their lips brushed. Just barely skimmed, but a crackle shot through her so tangibly she could have sworn the storm had returned with a bolt of lightning.

Gasping, she angled back, her eyes wide, his inscrutable.

"Um." She inched along the riser. "I need to get Evie, and um, thank you."

She shot to her feet, racing toward her daughter, away from the temptation to test the feeling and kiss him again.

That wasn't what she'd expected. At all. But then nothing about Whit had ever been predictable, damn his sexy body, hot kiss and hero's rescue.

# Sheltered by the Millionaire

## CATHERINE MANN

MILLS
BOON®
™

First published in Great Britain 2014
by Mills & Boon, an imprint of Harlequin (UK) Limited,
Large Print edition 2014
Eton House, 18-24 Paradise Road,
Richmond, Surrey, TW9 1SR

© 2014 Harlequin Books S.A.

Special thanks and acknowledgement are given
to Catherine Mann for her contribution to the
*Texas Cattleman's Club: After the Storm* miniseries.

ISBN: 978-0-263-24440-3

## CATHERINE MANN

*USA TODAY* bestselling author Catherine Mann lives on a sunny Florida beach with her flyboy husband and their four children. With more than forty books in print in over twenty countries, she has also celebrated wins for both a RITA® Award and a Booksellers' Best Award. Catherine enjoys chatting with readers online—thanks to the wonders of the internet, which allows her to network with her laptop by the water! Contact Catherine through her website, www.catherinemann.com, find her on Facebook and Twitter (@CatherineMann1), or reach her by snail mail at P.O. Box 6065, Navarre, FL 32566.

To my parents,
Brice and Sandra Woods.
Thank you for the joyous gift of
always having pets in my life as a child.

# One

The airbag inflated. Hard. Fast.

Pain exploded through Megan Maguire. From the bag hitting her in the face. From her body slamming against the seat. But it wasn't nearly as excruciating as the panic pumping through her as she faced the latest obstacle in reaching her daughter after a tornado.

A *tornado* for God's sake.

Her insides quivered with fear and her body ached from the impact. The wind howled outside her small compact car on the lonely street, eerily abandoned for 4:30 on a weekday afternoon. Apparently she was the only one stupid enough to keep driving in spite of the weather warnings of a tornado nearby. In fact, reports of the twister only made her more determined. She had to get to her daughter.

Megan punched her way clear of the deflating airbag to find a shattered windshield. The paw-shaped air freshener still swayed, dangling from her rearview mirror and releasing a hint of lavender. Files from work were scattered all over the floor from sliding off the seat along with the bag containing her daughter's Halloween costume. Then Megan looked outside and she damn near hyperventilated.

The hood of her sedan was covered by a downed tree. Steam puffed from the engine.

If the thick oak had fallen two seconds later, it would have landed on the roof of her car. She could have been crushed. She could have died.

Worst of all, her daughter would have become an orphan for all intents and purposes since Evie's father had never wanted anything to do with her. Panic pushed harder on Megan's chest like a cement slab.

Forcing oxygen back into her lungs one burning gasp at a time, she willed her racing heart to slow. Nothing would stop her from getting to her daughter. Not a totaled car. Not a downed tree. And definitely not…a…panic…attack.

Gasping for air, she flung open the door and stepped into the aftermath of the storm. Sheeting rain and storm winds battered her. Thank heaven she'd already left work to pick up her daughter for a special outing before they announced the tornado warning on her radio. If she'd been at the shelter when the warning sirens went off she wouldn't have been able to leave until given the okay.

But if she'd left at 1:00 to go to the movie as they'd originally planned, Evie would have been with her, safe and sound.

As a single mom, Megan needed her job as an animal shelter director. Evie's father had hit the road the minute Megan had told him about the unexpected pregnancy. Any attempts at child support had been ignored until he faded from sight somewhere in the Florida Keys. She'd finally accepted he was gone from her life and Evie's. She could only count on herself.

Determination fueled her aching body. She was less than a mile from her daughter's Little Tots Daycare. She would walk every step of the way if she had to. Rain plastered her khakis and work shirt to her body. Thank goodness her job called for casual wear. She would have been hard pressed to climb over the downed tree in heels.

At least the tornado had passed, but others could finger down from the gathering clouds at any minute. With every fiber of her being she prayed the worst was over. She had to get to her daughter, to be sure she was safe.

The small cottage that housed Little Tots Daycare had appeared so cute and appealing when she'd chosen it for Evie. Now, she could only think how insubstantial the structure would be against the force of such a strong storm. What if Evie was trapped inside?

Sweeping back a clump of soggy red hair, Megan clambered over the tree trunk and back onto the road strewn with debris. She took in the devastation ahead, collapsed buildings and overturned cars. The town had been spun and churned, pieces of everyday life left lining the street. Glass from blown-out windows. Papers and furniture from businesses. Pictures and books. The tornado's path was clear, like a massive mower had cut through the land. Uprooting trees, slicing through lives, spewing a roof or a computer like it was nothing more than a blade of grass sliced and swept away.

She picked her way past half of a splintered door. Wind whistled through the trees, bending and creaking the towering oaks. But she didn't hear the telltale train sound that preceded a tornado.

Thoughts of Evie scared and waiting dumped acid on Megan's gut. Even knowing the Little Tots Daycare workers were equipped to handle the crisis didn't quell her fears. Evie was her daughter.

Her world.

She would trudge through this storm, tear her way through the wreckage, do anything to reach her four-year-old child. The roar of the wind was calling to her, urging her forward until she could have sworn she actually heard someone speaking to her. *Megan. Megan. Megan.* Had she sustained a concussion from the wreck?

She searched around her, pushing her shoulder-length hair from her face, and spotted a handful of people every bit as reckless as her venturing outside for one reason or another. None of them looked her way…except for a looming man, a familiar man, charging down the steps of one of the many buildings owned by Daltry Property Management. For three and a half years, Whit Daltry had been a major pain in the neck whenever they'd crossed paths, which she tried to make as infrequently as possible.

The fates were really ganging up on her today.

Whit shouted, "Megan? Megan! Come inside before you get hurt."

"No," she shouted. "I can't."

His curse rode the wind as he jogged toward her. Tall and muscular, a force to be reckoned with, he plowed ahead, his Stetson impervious to the wind. Raindrops sheeted off the brim of his hat, as his suit coat and tie whipped to and fro.

He stopped alongside her, his brown eyes snapping with anger, warm hand clasping her arm. "I couldn't believe it when I saw you through the window. What are you doing out in this weather?"

"Dancing in the rain," she snapped back, hysteria threatening to overwhelm her. "What do you think I'm doing? I'm trying to get to Evie. I had already left the shelter when the tornado hit. A tree fell on my car so I had to walk."

His jaw flexed, his eyes narrowing. "Where is your daughter?"

She tugged her arm free. "She's at Little Tots Daycare. I have to go to her."

And what a time to remember this man was the very reason she didn't work closer to her daughter's preschool. When the shelter had decided to build a new facility shortly after she'd signed on as director three and a half years ago, Whit had started off their acquaintance by blocking the purchase of land near his offices—which also happened to be near the day care. The Safe Haven's board of directors had been forced to choose an alternate location. Now the shelter was located in a more industrial area farther from her daughter. Every single work day, Megan lost time with Evie because of an arbitrary decision by this man.

And now, he could have cost her so much more if something had happened to Evie.

Whit grasped her arms again, more firmly this time, peering at her from under the brim of his hat. "I'll get your daughter. You need to take shelter until the weather clears. There could be more tornadoes."

"You don't know me very well if you think I'll even entertain that idea." She grabbed his suit coat lapels. "There's no way I'm sitting in a gas station bathroom hugging my knees and covering my head while my Evie is out there scared. She's probably crying for me."

"Look at the roads—" He waved to the street full of branches and overturned vehicles. "They're blocked here too. Only a truck or heavy-duty SUV would stand a chance of getting through."

"I'll run, walk or crawl my way there. It's not that much farther."

He bit off another curse and scrubbed his strong jaw with one hand. "Fine. If I can't convince you, then we might as well get moving. Hopefully, my truck can four-wheel it over the debris and drive that last two blocks a lot faster than you can walk. Are you okay with that?"

"Seriously? Yes. Let's go." Relief soaked into her, nearly buckling her knees.

Whit led her back to the redbrick building and into the parking garage, his muscular arm along her back helping her forge ahead. Time passed in a fugue as she focused on one thing. Seeing her daughter.

Thumbing the key remote, Whit unlocked the large blue truck just ahead of them and started the engine from outside the truck. She ran the last few steps, yanked open the passenger door and crawled inside the top-of-the-line vehicle, surprisingly clean for a guy, with no wrenches or files or gym bag on the floor. No child's Halloween costume or box of recycling like what she had in her destroyed car, and— Oh, God, her mind was on overdrive from adrenaline. The warmth of the heater blasted over her wet body. Her teeth chattered. From the cold or shock? She wasn't sure and didn't care.

She could only think of her child. "Thank you for doing this, Whit."

"We may have had our differences, but these are extraordinary circumstances." He looked at her intensely for an instant as he set his hat on the seat between them. "Your daughter will be fine. That day care building may look small but it's rock solid, completely up to code. And that's me speaking as a professional in property management."

"I understand that in my mind." Megan tapped her temple. "But in my heart?" Her hand trembled as it fluttered to her chest. "The fears and what-ifs can't be quieted."

"You're a mother. That's understandable." He shifted the truck into four-wheel drive and accelerated out of the parking lot, crunching over debris, cracked concrete and churned earth. "How did the shelter fare in the storm?"

Her gut clenched all over again as she thought of all the precious charges in her care. "I wasn't there. I'd already left to pick up Evie when the warning siren went off. The kennel supervisor is in charge and I trust him, completely, but telephone service is out."

She felt torn in two. But she had a stellar staff

in place at the shelter. They were trained to respond and rescue in disaster scenarios. She'd just never expected to use that training to find her child.

Already the rain was easing, the storm passing as quickly as it had hit. Such a brief time for so much change to happen. And there could be worse waiting for her—

The worst.

Her chin trembled, tears of panic nearly choking her. "I was supposed to take the whole afternoon off to go to a movie with Evie, but we had a sick employee leave early and a mother dog in labor dumped off with us… If I had kept my promise I would have been at the afternoon matinee with Evie rather than copping out for a later show. God, she must be so terrified—" She pressed her wrist to her mouth to hold back a sob.

"You can't torture yourself with what-ifs," he said matter-of-factly. "There was no way to see this coming and no way to know where it would be safe. You were doing your job, supporting your child. Deep breaths. Be calm for your kid."

She scrubbed her wrist under her eyes. "You're

right. She'll be more frightened if she sees me freaking out."

Whit turned the corner onto the street for the Little Tots Daycare. The one-story wooden cottage was still standing but had sustained significant damage.

The aluminum roof was crunched like an accordion, folded in on the wooden porch. Already other parents and a couple of volunteer emergency responders were picking through the rubble. The porch supports had fallen like broken matches, the thick wooden beams cracked and splintered so that the main entrance was completely blocked.

Megan's heart hit her shoes.

Before she could find her breath, Whit had already jogged to her side of the truck and opened the door.

"No," she choked out a whisper. She fell into his arms, her legs weak with fear, her whole body stiff from the accident. Pain shot up her wrists where, she realized, she had burns from the airbag deployment.

None of it mattered. Her eyes focused on that

fallen roof. The blocked door. More acid churned in her stomach as she thought of her little girl stuck inside.

"I've got you," Whit reassured her, rain dripping from the brim of his Stetson.

"I'm okay. You can let go. I have to find my daughter."

"And I'm going to help you do that. I have construction experience and we need to be careful our help doesn't cause more damage."

No wonder the other parents weren't tearing apart the fallen debris to get inside.

"Of course, you're right." Hands quaking, she pressed a palm to her forehead. "I'm sorry. I'm not thinking clearly."

"That's understandable. We'll get to your daughter soon. You have my word."

Whit led her past the debris of the front porch, then around to the side, where the swing sets were uprooted, the jungle gym twisted into a macabre new shape. Painted Halloween pumpkins had scattered and burst. He called out to the handful of people picking at the lumber on the porch, offering advice as he continued to lead

Megan around to the back of the building. The gaggle of frantic parents listened without argument, desperate.

She couldn't imagine a world without her daughter.

In her first trimester, she'd planned to give her baby up for adoption. She'd gotten the paperwork from a local adoption agency. Then she'd felt the flutter of life inside her and she'd torn up the paperwork. From that point on, she'd opted for taking life one day at a time. The moment when she'd seen her daughter's newborn face with bright eyes staring trustingly up at her, she'd lost her heart totally.

Evie was four years old now, those first sprigs of red hair having grown into precious corkscrew curls. And Megan had a rewarding job that also paid the bills and supported her daughter. It hadn't been easy by any stretch, but she'd managed. Until today.

Whit guided her to the back of the building, which was blessedly undamaged. The back door was intact. Secure. Safe. She'd been right to come with him. She would have dived straight into the porch rubble rather than thinking to check....

Megan yanked out of Whit's grip and pounded on the door. Through the pane she could see the kids lined up on the floor with their teachers. No one seemed in a panic.

The day care supervisor pulled the door open.

"Sue Ellen," Megan clasped her hand, looking around her to catch sight of her daughter. "Where's Evie?"

"She's okay." The silver-haired supervisor wearing a smock covered in finger paints and dust patted Megan's hand. The older woman seemed calm, in control, when she must be shaking in her sensible white sneakers. "She's with a teacher's assistant and three other students. They were on their way to the kitchen when the tornado sirens went off. So she's at the other end of the building."

Sue Ellen paused and Megan's heart tripped over itself. "What are you not telling me?"

"There's a beam from the roof blocking her from coming out. But she's fine. The assistant is keeping the kids talking and calm."

Megan pressed a hand to her chest. "Near the porch? The collapsed roof?"

Whit gripped her shoulder. "I've got it."

Without another word, he raced down the corridor. Megan followed, dimly registering that he'd clasped her hand. And she didn't pull away from the comfort. They finally stopped short at a blocked hall, the emergency lighting illuminating the passageway beyond the crisscross of broken beams and cracked plaster. Dust made the image hazy, almost surreal. The teacher's assistant sat beside the row of students, Evie on the end, her bright red curls as unmistakable as the mismatched orange and purple outfit she'd insisted on wearing this morning because the colors reminded her Halloween was coming.

"Evie?" Megan shouted. "Evie, honey, it's Mommy."

"Mommy?" her daughter answered faintly, a warble in her voice. "I wanna go home."

Whit angled past Megan and crouched down to assess the crisscross of boards, cracked drywall and ceiling tiles. 'Stand back, kids, while I clear a path through."

The teacher's assistant guided them all a few feet away and wrapped her arms around them protectively as fresh dust showered down. With measured precision, Whit moved boards aside, his muscles bulging as he hefted aside plank after plank with an ease Megan envied until finally he'd cleared a pathway big enough for people to crawl through. Evie's freckled face peeked from the cluster of kids, her nose scrunched and sweet cherub smile beaming. She appeared unharmed.

Relief made Megan's legs weak. Whit's palm slid along her waist for a steadying second before he reached into the two-foot opening, arms outstretched. "Evie, I'm a friend of your mommy's here to help you. Can I lift you through here?"

Megan nodded, holding back the tears that were welling up fast. "Go to Mr. Whit, honey."

Evie raised her arms and Whit hauled her up and free, cradling her to his chest in broad, gentle hands. Megan took in every inch of her daughter, seeing plenty of dirt but nothing more than a little tear of one sleeve of her Disney princess shirt, revealing a tiny scrape. Somehow she'd come through the whole ordeal safely.

Once they reached the bottom of the rubble, Whit passed Evie to her mother. "Here ya go, kiddo."

Evie melted against Megan with one of those shuddering sighs of relief that relayed more than tears how frightened she had been. Evie wrapped her tiny arms around Megan's neck and held on tightly like a spider monkey, and it was Megan's turn to feel the shudder of relief so strong she nearly fell to her knees.

*Thank you, thank you, thank you, God.* Her baby was safe.

"You're okay, sweetie?"

"I'm fine, Mommy. The t'naydo came and I was a very brave girl. I did just what Miss Vicky told me to do. I sat under the stairs and hugged my knees tight with one arm and I held my friend Caitlyn's hand 'cause she was scared."

"You did well, Evie, I'm so proud of you." She kissed her daughter's forehead, taking in the hint of her daughter's favorite raspberry shampoo. "I love you so much."

"Love you, too, Mommy." She squeezed hard,

holding on tightly as Whit helped the other students through.

Once the last child stepped free, Whit urged everyone to file away from the damaged part of the building. He led them down the hall to where Sue Ellen had gathered the children in the auditorium, playing music and passing out cookies and books to the students whose parents hadn't arrived to pick them up. The school nurse made the rounds checking each child, dispensing Band-Aids when needed.

Whit's hand went to the small of Megan's back again with an ease she didn't have the energy to wonder about right now.

"Megan, you should see the nurse about your scratches from the accident. The air bag has left some burns that could use antiseptic too—"

She shook her head. "I will later. For now she's got her hands full with the children and they need her more."

Evie squirmed in her arms. "Can I get a cookie? I'm reallllly hungry."

"Of course, sweetie." She gave her daughter

another hug, not sure when she would ever be okay with letting her out of her sight.

Evie raced across the gym floor as if the whole world hadn't just been blown upside down. Literally.

Whit laughed softly. "Resilient little scrap."

"More so than her mom, I'm afraid." Megan sagged and sat down on the metal riser.

"All Evie knows is that everyone is okay and you're here." Whit sat beside her, his leg pressing a warm reassurance against hers. "Maybe we should get you one of those cookies and a cup of that juice."

"I'm okay. Really. We should go back to clearing the debris outside." She braced her shoulders. "I'm being selfish in keeping you all to myself."

"All the children are accounted for and the teachers have them well in hand. It's getting dark. I think cleanup will be on hold until the morning."

What kind of carnage would the morning reveal? Outside, sirens had wailed for the last twenty minutes. "I should take Evie and check back in at the shelter. Local animal control will need our help with housing displaced pets."

"Civilians aren't allowed on the road just yet and you don't have a car." He nudged her with his shoulder. "Face it, Megan. You can actually afford to take a few minutes to catch your breath."

The concern in his brown eyes was genuine. The warmth she saw there washed over her like a jolt of pure java, stimulating her senses. Why hadn't she ever noticed before what incredibly intense and expressive eyes he had? Sure, she'd noticed he was sexy, but then any woman who crossed his path would appreciate Whit Daltry's charismatic good looks. And in fact, that had been a part of what turned her off for the past three years—how easily women fell into his arms. She'd let herself be conned by a man like that and it had turned her life upside down.

But the warmth in his eyes now, the caring he'd shown in helping her get to Evie today presented a new side to Whit she'd never seen before. He might not be romance material for her, but he'd been a good guy just now and that meant a lot to a woman who didn't accept help easily.

She slumped back against the riser behind her. "Thank you for what you did for me today—for me and for Evie. I know you would have done the same for anyone stranded on the road." As she said the words she realized they were true. Whit wasn't the one-dimensional bad guy she'd painted him to be the past few years. There were layers to the man. "Still, the fact is, you were there for my child and I'll never forget that."

He smiled, his brown eyes twinkling with a hint of his devilish charm. "Does that mean I'm forgiven for refusing to let the shelter build on that tract of land you wanted so much?"

Layers. Definitely. Good—and bad. "I may be grateful, but I didn't develop amnesia."

He chuckled, a low rumble that drew a laugh from her, and before she knew what she was doing, she dropped her hand to his shoulder and squeezed.

"Thank you." She leaned to kiss his cheek in a heartfelt thank-you just as he turned to answer.

Their lips brushed. Just barely skimmed, but a crackle shot through her so tangibly she could have sworn the storm had returned with a bolt of lightning.

Gasping, she angled back, her eyes wide, his inscrutable.

She inched along the riser. "I need to get Evie… and um, thank you."

She shot to her feet, racing toward her daughter, away from the temptation to test the feeling and kiss him again.

That wasn't what she'd expected. At all. But then nothing about Whit had ever been predictable, damn his sexy body, hot kiss and hero's rescue. She'd been every bit as gullible as her mother once. And while she could never regret having Evie in her life, she damn well wouldn't fall victim to trusting an unworthy man again. She owed it to Evie to set a better example, to break the cycle the women in her family seemed destined to repeat.

And if that meant giving up any chance for another toe-searing kiss from Whit Daltry, then so be it.

# Two

*Six Weeks Later*

The wild she-cat in his arms left scratches on his shoulders.

Whit Daltry adjusted his hold on the long-haired calico, an older female kitten that had wandered—scraggly and with no collar—onto the doorstep of his Pine Valley home. Luckily, he happened to know the very attractive director of Royal's Safe Haven Animal Shelter.

He stepped out of his truck and kicked the door closed, early morning sunshine reflecting off his windshield. Not a cloud in the sky, unlike that fateful day the F4 tornado had ripped through Royal, Texas. The shelter had survived unscathed, but the leaves had been stripped from the trees, leaving branches unnaturally bare for this region of Texas, even in November. The town bore lasting scars from that day that would take a lot longer to heal than the scratches from the frantic calico.

He should have gotten one of those pet carriers or a box to transport the cat. If the beast clawed its way out of his arms, chances were the scared feline would bolt away and be tough as hell to catch again. Apparently he wasn't adept at animal rescue.

That was Megan's expertise.

The thought of seeing her again sent anticipation coursing through him as each step brought him closer to the single-story brick structure. Heaven knew he could use a distraction from life right now. For six weeks, ever since they'd shared that kiss after the tornado, he'd been looking for an excuse to see her, but the town had been in chaos clearing the debris. Some of his properties had been damaged as well. He owned multiple apartment buildings and rental homes all over town. And while he might have a light-hearted approach to his social life, he was serious when it came to business and was always damn sure going to be there for his tenants when they needed him.

He'd thrown himself into the work to distract himself from the biggest loss of all—the death of his good friend Craig Richardson in the storm. It had sent him into shock for the first couple of weeks, as he grieved for Craig and tried to find ways to help his pal's widow. God, they were all still in a tailspin and he didn't know if he would be in any better shape by the memorial service that was scheduled for after Thanksgiving.

So he focused on restoring order to the town, the only place he'd ever called home after a root-less childhood being evicted from place after place. And with each clean-up operation, he thought back to the day of the storm, to clearing aside the rubble in the day care.

To Megan's kiss afterward.

Sure the kiss had been impulsive and motivated by gratitude, and she'd meant to land it on his cheek. But he would bet good money that she'd been every bit as affected by the spontaneous kiss as he was.

Granted, he'd always been attracted to her in spite of their sparring. But he'd managed to keep a tight rein on those feelings for the three and a half years he'd known her because she'd made it clear she found him barely one step above pond scum. Now, he couldn't ignore the possibility that the chemistry was mutual. So finally, here he was. He had the perfect excuse, even if it wasn't the perfect time.

And Megan wouldn't be able to avoid him as she'd been doing since their clash over the site where she'd wanted the new shelter built. A battle he'd won. Although from the sleek look of the Safe Haven facility, she'd landed on her feet and done well for the homeless four-legged residents of Royal, Texas.

Tucking the cat into his suit coat and securing her with a firm grip, he stepped into the welcoming reception area, its tiled surfaces giving off a freshly washed bleach smell. The waiting area was spacious, but today, there were wire crates lining two walls, one with cats, the other with small dogs. They were clean and neat, but the shelter was packed to capacity. He'd heard the shelter had taken in a large number of strays displaced during the storm, but he hadn't fully grasped the implications until now.

The shelter had a reputation for its innovative billboards, slogans and holiday-themed decor, but right now, every ounce of energy here seemed to be focused on keeping the animals fed and the place sparkling clean.

He closed the door, sealing himself inside.

The cat sunk her claws in deeper. Whit hissed almost as loudly as the feline and searched the space for help. Framed posters featured everything from collages of adopters to advice on flea prevention. Painted red-and-black paw prints marked the walls with directions he already knew in theory since he'd reviewed the plans during his land dispute with Megan.

A grandmotherly woman sat behind the counter labeled "volunteer receptionist." He recognized the retired legal secretary from past business ventures. She was texting on her phone, and waved for him to wait an instant before she glanced up.

He swept his hat off and set it on the counter. "Morning, Miss Abigail—"

"Good mornin', Whit," the lady interrupted with a particularly thick Southern accent, her eyes widening with surprise. The whole town knew he and Megan avoided each other like the plague. "What a pleasant surprise you've decided to adopt from us. Our doggies are housed to your right in kennel runs. But be sure to peek at the large fenced-in area outside. Volunteers take them there to exercise in the grassy area."

She paused for air, but not long enough for him to get in a word. "Although now I see you're a cat person. Never would have guessed that." She grinned as the calico peeked out of his suit jacket, purring as if the ferocious feline hadn't drawn blood seconds earlier. "Kitties are kept in our free roam area. If you find one you would like to adopt, we have meet-and-greet rooms for your sweetheart there to meet with your new feline friend—"

"I'm actually here to make a donation." He

hadn't planned on that, but given all the extra crates, he could see the shelter needed help. So much of the post-tornado assistance had been focused on helping people and cleaning up the damaged buildings. But he should have realized the repercussions of the storm would have a wider ripple effect.

"A donation?" Miss Abigail set aside her phone. "Let me call our director right away—oh, here she is now."

He pivoted to find Megan walking down the dog corridor, toward the lobby, a beagle on a loose leash at her side. He could see the instant she registered his presence. She blinked fast, nibbling her lip as she paused midstep for an instant before forging ahead, the sweet curves of her hips sending a rush of want through him.

Her bright red hair was pulled back in a low ponytail. He ached to sweep away that gold clasp and thread his fingers through the fiery strands, to find out if her hair was as silky as it looked. He wanted her, had since the first time he'd seen her when they crossed paths in the lawyer's office during the dispute over a patch of property.

He'd expected to smooth things over regarding finding an alternate location for the new shelter. He usually had no trouble charming people, but she'd taken to disliking him right away. Apparently her negative impression had only increased every time she perceived one of his projects as "damaging" to nature when he purchased a piece of wetlands.

He'd given up trying to figure out why she couldn't see her way clear to making nice. Because she had a reputation for being everyone's pal, a caring and kindhearted woman who took in strays of all kinds, ready to pitch in to help anyone. Except for him.

"Megan," the receptionist cleared her throat, "Mr. Daltry here has brought us a donation."

"Another cat. Just what we were lacking." Megan's smile went tight.

He juggled his hold on the fractious fur ball. "I do plan to write a check to cover the expense of taking in another animal, but yes, I need to drop off the stray. She's been wandering around in the woods near my house. She doesn't have a collar and clearly hasn't been eating well."

"Could have been displaced because of the storm and has been surviving on her own in the wild ever since, poor girl. Animals have a knack for ditching their collars. Did you take her to a vet to check for a microchip?"

"I figured you could help me with that. Or maybe someone has come by here looking for her."

"So you're sure it's a girl?"

"I think so."

"Let's just pray she's not in heat or about to have kittens."

Oh, crap. He hadn't thought about that.

Megan passed him the dog leash and took the squirming cat from his arms. Their wrists brushed in the smooth exchange. A hint of her cinnamon scent drifted by, teasing him with memories of that too-brief kiss a month ago.

She swallowed hard once; it was the only sign she'd registered the brief contact, aside from the fact that she kept her eyes firmly averted from his. What would he see in those emerald-green eyes? A month ago, after her impulsive kiss, he'd seen surprise—and desire.

He watched her every move, trying to get a read on her.

"Hey, beautiful," she crooned to the kitty, handling the feline with obvious skill and something more…an unmistakable gift. "Let's get a scanner and check to see if you have a chip. If we're lucky, you'll have your people back very soon."

Kneeling, she pulled a brown, boxy device from under the counter and waved the sensor along the back of the cat's neck. She frowned and swept it over the same place again. Then she broadened the search along the cat's shoulders and legs, casting a quick glance at Whit. "Sometimes the chip migrates on the body."

But after sweeping along the cat's entire back, Megan shook her head and sighed. "No luck."

"She was pretty matted when I found her yesterday." He patted the beagle's head awkwardly. He didn't have much experience with pets, his only exposure to animals coming with horseback riding. The cat and dog were a helluva lot smaller than a Palomino. "I combed her out last night and she's been pissed at me ever since."

She glanced up quickly, her eyes going wide with surprise. "You brushed the cat?"

"Yeah, so?" He shrugged. "She needed it."

Her forehead furrowed. "That was kind of you."

"Last time I checked, I'm not a monster."

She smiled with a tinge of irony. "Just a mogul land baron and destroyer of wetlands."

He raised a hand. "Guilty as charged. And I hear you have need of some of my dirty, land-baron dollars?"

He looked around, taking in a couple of harried volunteers rushing in with fresh litter boxes stacked in their arms. The dog sniffed his shoes as if checking out the quality of his next chew toy.

The stuffing went out of her fight and she sagged back against the wall. "Animal control across town is full, and we're the only other option around here. People are living in emergency housing shelters that don't allow pets. Other folks have left town altogether, just giving up on finding their animals." He could hear the tension in her voice.

"That's a damn shame, Megan. I've heard the

call-outs for pet food, but I hadn't realized how heavy the extra burden is for you and the rest of your staff."

"Let's step into my office before your kitty girl makes a break for the door. Evie's in there now, but it'll only take a second to settle her elsewhere so we can talk." She rested a hand on the front desk. "Miss Abigail, do you mind if Evie sits with you for a few minutes?"

"Of course not. I love spending time with the little darlin'. You don't let me babysit near enough. Send her my way."

Megan looked at Whit, something sad flickering in her eyes. "Evie's taking the day off from school. Come this way."

He followed her, his eyes drawn to the gentle sway of her hips. Khaki had never looked so hot. "I'm sorry to add to your load here, but I meant it when I said I want to make a donation to help."

She opened a metal baby gate and ushered the beagle into the room. It was a small room with a neat bookshelf and three recycling bins stacked in a corner. Two large framed watercolors dominated the walls—one of an orange cat and the other of a spotted dog, both clearly painted by a child. The bottom corner of each was signed in crayon. *Evie.*

The little minx peeked from under the desk, a miniature version of her mom right down to the freckles on her nose. "Hello, Mr. Whit."

She crawled out with an iPad tucked under her arm, then stood, her red pigtails lopsided. Evie's face was one hundred percent Megan, but the little girl had a quirky spirit all her own. Evie wore a knight's costume with a princess tiara even though Halloween had already passed and Thanksgiving was rapidly approaching. Her mother smoothed a hand over her head affectionately, gently tightening the left pigtail to match the one on the right. "Miss Abigail wants you to sit with her for a few minutes, okay? I'll be through soon."

Evie waved shyly, green eyes sparkling, then sprinted out to the front desk, carrying her iPad and a foam sword.

Megan gestured for him to step inside the small office, then closed the gate again. "You mentioned writing a check, and I'm not bashful about accepting on behalf of the animals. I'll get you a receipt so you can write it off on your taxes."

"Where will you put this cat if you're already full?" he asked as the beagle sniffed his shoes.

"I guess we'll learn if she gets along with dogs since she'll have to stay in my office for now." She crouched down with the cat in her arms. The pup tipped his head to the side and the cat curled closer to Megan but kept her claws sheathed. Nodding, Megan stood and settled the cat onto her office chair.

"She likes dogs better than she likes me, that's for sure." He shook his head, laughing softly.

"I guess not every female in this town likes crawling into your arms." She crinkled her freckled nose.

He would have thought she was jealous. She *had* been avoiding him since the tornado. He would have attributed it to her being busy with cleanup, but his instincts shouted it had something to do with that impulsive kiss. "I feel bad for adding to your load here. Could you use more volunteers to help with the extra load here? I'm sure some of my buddies at the Texas Cattleman's Club would be glad to step up."

"We can always use extra hands."

"I'll contact Gil Addison—the club president— and get the ball rolling. Maybe they'll adopt when they're here."

"We can only hope." Her hand fell to the cat's head and she stroked lightly. The cat arched up into the stroke, purring loudly. "I'm working on arranging a transport for some of the unclaimed pets to a rescue in Oklahoma. A group in Colorado has reached out to help as well, but we're still trying to find a way to get the animals there. And since the Colorado group is a new rescue, I need to look over their operation before entrusting our animals to their care. Except I don't know how I'll be able to take off that much time from work for the road trip, much less be away from Evie for that long. She's still unsettled from the trauma of last month's storm. But, well, you don't need to hear all about my troubles."

"My personal plane is at your disposal," he said without hesitation.

"What? I didn't realize you have a plane. I mean I know you're well off, but…."

Her shoulders braced and he could almost see another wall appearing between them. He appreciated that she wasn't impressed by his money, but also hated to see another barrier in place.

Still, the more he thought about flying the animals for her, the more the idea appealed to him. "Make the arrangements with the rescue and whatever else needs to be done as far as crating the animals. I assume you have procedures for that."

"Yes, but…." Confusion creased her forehead. "I don't know how to say thank-you. That's going above and beyond."

"There's nothing to thank me for. This is a win-win." He got to help the animals, score points with Megan and spend more time with her to boot.

"But the cost—"

"A tax write-off, remember? Fly animals as far as you need them to go and your time away will be reduced considerably." This idea just got better and better, not only for the animals, but also by giving him an "in" to see Megan, to figure out where to take this attraction. "This isn't a one-time offer either. You're packed with critters here. If there's help out there, take it and my jet will fly them there."

"I can't turn you down. The animals need this kind of miracle if we're going to find homes for them by the holidays." She exhaled hard. "I need to get to work placing calls. There are rescues I hadn't considered before because of the distance and our limited resources. Rescue work happens fast, slots fill up at a moment's notice."

"And this little gal?" He stroked the cat's head and for once the calico didn't dig her claws in. Perched on the back of the chair, she arched up into his hand and purred like a race car.

"Are you sure you don't want to keep her?"

He pulled his hand away. "I can't. I'm at work all the time, which wouldn't be fair to her."

"Of course." Megan looked disappointed in him, even though he'd just offered her thousands of dollars' worth of flight hours.

But then, hadn't he said it? Offering his plane was easy. Taking care of another living being? Not so easy.

"I should let you get to work on lining up those rescues." He pulled a business card from his wallet and plucked a pen from the cup on the edge of her desk. He jotted a number on the back of the card. "This is my private cell number and my secretary's number. Don't hesitate to call."

When he passed her the card, their fingers brushed. He saw the flecks of awareness sparkle in her eyes again. He wasn't mistaken. The mutual draw was real, but now wasn't the time to press ahead for more.

"Thank you again." She flipped the card between her fingers, still watching him with suspicion, their old conflicts clearly making her wary. "Would you like to name your kitty cat?"

"That's not my kitten."

"Right," she answered, a smile playing with her plump lips that didn't need makeup to entice, "and she still needs a name. We've had to name so many this past month, we're out of ideas."

He thought for a second then found himself saying, "Tallulah."

"Tallulah?" Her surprise was a reward. He

liked unsettling her. "Really, Whit? I didn't expect such a…girly name choice."

"That was the name of my mom's cat." She was briefly theirs, but when they'd moved, the cat ran away. Then his father had said no more pets. Period.

"It's a lovely name."

He nodded quickly then turned to leave.

"Whit," she called, stopping him short, "about what happened after you helped me get to Evie that day…."

Was she finally acknowledging the impulsive, explosive kiss? The thought of having her sooner rather than later… "Yes?"

"Thank you for helping me reach my daughter." She looked down at her shoes for an awkward moment before meeting his eyes again. "I can never repay you for that…and now this."

"I don't expect repayment." The last thing he wanted was to have her kiss him again out of gratitude.

The next time they kissed—and there would be a next time—it would be purely based on mutual attraction.

* * *

The stroke of Whit Daltry's eyes left her skin tingling.

Standing at the shelter's glass door, Megan rubbed her arms as she watched Whit stride across the parking lot back to his truck. His long legs ate up the space one powerful step at a time. His suit coat flapped in the late afternoon breeze revealing a too-perfect, taut butt. Her head was still reeling from his surprise appearance, followed by the generous offer she couldn't turn down.

After six weeks of reliving that brief but mind-blowing kiss, she'd seen him again and would be spending an entire day with him. Somehow, because of that day they'd gone from avoiding each other to.... What? She wasn't sure exactly.

Maybe he'd gotten the wrong idea from that kiss and thought she was looking for something more. But she didn't have time in her life for more. She had a demanding job and a daughter, and both had taken a hard hit from last month's tornado.

And speaking of her child, she'd left Evie long

enough. Thank goodness Miss Abigail had been so accommodating about helping with Evie. The retired legal secretary had even babysat a couple of evenings when Megan got called out to assist with an emergency rescue. Evie had been particularly clingy this past month. And she couldn't blame her. That nightmarish day still haunted Megan as well; she often woke up from dreams of not reaching her daughter in time, of the whole roof of the preschool collapsing.

Dreams that sometimes took a different turn with Whit arriving, of the kiss going further....

Megan watched his truck drive away, a knot in her stomach.

It would be too damn easy to lean on those broad shoulders, to get used to the help, which would only make things more difficult when she was on her own again. Megan turned away from the door and temptation, returning to reality in the form of her precious daughter sitting on Abigail's lap as they played on the iPad together. Evie's knight's armor was slipping off one shoulder, her toy sword on the ground beside her tiara.

Megan held out her arms. "Come here, sweetie."

She gathered Evie into her arms and held her on her hip. Not much longer and her baby girl would be too big to carry around. This precious child, who wanted to be a "princess knight" for Halloween and cut through tornadoes with a foam sword. Megan had hoped her daughter would relax and heal as they put the storm behind them, but now Thanksgiving was approaching and Evie was still showing signs of trauma.

The holidays were tough anyway, reminding her that she was the sole relative in Evie's life. She was a thirty-year-old single mom.

And damn lucky to have landed in this small town full of warmhearted friends.

"Thank you, Abigail, for helping out even after the school finished repairs. You've been a lifesaver."

The roof of Little Tots Daycare had been reconstructed quickly, but the dust and stress had taken its toll on the kids and the workers. Some had gotten the flu.

Others, like Evie, had nightmares and begged to stay home. Her daughter conquered pretend monsters in iPad games and dress-up play.

Abigail rocked back in her chair. "My pleasure. She's a doll." She pinched Evie's cheek lightly. "We have fun readin' books on the iPad. Don't we, Evie?"

Bringing her daughter to work wasn't optimal, but Megan didn't have any choices for now. "Thanks again."

"I'm always a call away. The benefit of being retired. Maybe we'll see Mr. Daltry again tomorrow. Now wouldn't that be nice if he became a regular volunteer?"

As much as Megan wanted to keep her distance, she couldn't ignore all the amazing things Whit had done for her.

Evie patted her mother's cheek with a tiny palm. "Where did the nice man go?"

"He brought a kitty to stay with us here."

She stuck out her bottom lip. "We don't like people who dump their pets. Does this mean I can't like him anymore?"

"He didn't dump the kitty, sweetie. He saved her from being cold and hungry in the woods." Although she had to admit she was disappointed he hadn't offered to keep the cat. She struggled not to resent his wealthy lifestyle. Everyone knew he was a self-made man who'd worked hard to build a fortune before his thirty-fifth birthday. "Tallulah lost her family and had nowhere else to go. We're going to help her find them again."

"'Lulah?"

"Right. That's her name."

"She can come home wif us and live in our house. I'll get her a costume too."

They already had three cats and two dogs, all of which Evie had been dressing up as part of her medieval warrior team. The costumes transformed them into horses, elves, queens and even a unicorn.

Their house was full.

And Megan was at her limit with work and her daughter. "You can visit Tallulah here while she waits to find her family. We have our kitties and doggies at home to take care of and love."

Evie patted Megan's face again. "Don't worry, Mommy. I'll tell Mr. Whit to keep 'Lulah."

If only it worked that easily. "I need to work a little longer, just a few phone calls and then we can go home for supper. We'll make a pizza."

"Can Mr. Whit share our pizza?"

Abigail laughed softly from her perch behind the counter. "I think Mr. Whit wants to share a lot more than pizza."

Evie looked up, frowning. "Like what?"

Megan shot Abigail an exasperated look before kneeling to tell Evie, "Mr. Whit is sharing his airplane to help send some of the puppies and kitties to forever homes before Thanksgiving."

"He shares his plane? See. He is very nice. Can I play my games, please?" Evie squirmed down with her iPad, her foam sword tumbling from her hand. "I'm gonna play a plane game this time." Her daughter put on her tiara and fired up a game for touring the states in a puffy airplane.

Megan glanced at the receptionist. "I don't want to hear a word about Whit's visit today, Abigail. And no gossiping."

She glanced over her shoulder to see if other volunteers were listening in. Luckily, most of them were occupied with exercising animals, folding laundry and washing bowls. The only person even remotely close enough to hear was Beth Andrews, Megan's favorite volunteer.

"Gossip?" Beth chimed in. "Did I hear the word gossip? That would surely never happen in the town of Royal where everyone stays out of each other's business. Not."

Beth wasn't a known gossip, but was definitely known for helping out everywhere; she was very involved in the community. The leggy blonde owned Green Acres, a local organic farm and produce stand. Beth's business had taken a big hit from the tornado. That made her generosity and caring now all the more special, given how rough life had been for her lately. The homemade goodies she brought to the animals were always a treat. Beth had that willowy thin, effortless beauty that would have had women resenting her if it weren't for the fact she was so darn nice.

Abigail stroked her phone as if already planning a text. "It's a gift having a community that cares so much. Like how Whit Daltry just showed up to make a big donation."

Beth arched a blond eyebrow. "You two are speaking to each other?"

Megan shrugged her shoulders and examined her fingernails. "He's helping with the overflow of animals. I can work with anyone for the good of the animals."

"Everyone's had their lives turned upside down since the twister. To lose over a dozen lives in a blink…to have our friend Craig gone so young.…" She paused with a heavy sigh. "No one has been exempt from the fallout of this damn storm. Even our mayor was critically injured. And that poor Skye Taylor…"

"What tragic bad luck that she came back to town after four years on such a terrible day. How is she doing?" Megan rubbed her arms again, feeling petty for stressing over her life, thinking of Skye Taylor, found seriously injured and unconscious after the storm, her baby delivered prematurely. And since Skye was still in a coma, she hadn't even met her child. Megan shivered again, even though she didn't know the woman personally. As a mother, she felt a bond. Thank God Evie was safe. That's what mattered most. She would figure out how to heal her daughter's fears.

Clearly agitated, Beth thumbed a stack of shelter flyers. "Drew checked in with the family and

Skye is still in a medically induced coma and the baby girl—Grace—is in the neonatal intensive care unit."

Abigail sighed. "And the doctors still don't know who the father is?"

Did this qualify as gossip? Megan wasn't sure, but if the talk could help find the father, that would be a good thing. "I've never met her, but I heard a rumor Skye ran off with the younger Holt brother despite their parents' protests. So I assumed he was the dad."

Beth tucked a stray curl back into her loose topknot, scrunching her nose. "I recall hearing mentions of an age-old feud between the Holts and Taylors. Abigail, do you have any idea who started it?"

"I haven't a clue. Quite frankly, I'm not sure they do either, anymore."

Beth shook her head slowly. "How sad when feuds are carried on for so long." She stared pointedly at Megan. "So what's this with Whit Daltry coming to the shelter to see you? And you actually spoke to him rather than running out the back exit?"

"Running out the back? I wouldn't do that." Okay, so maybe she had avoided him a time or two but hearing it put that way made her sound so…wimpy. And she didn't like that one damn bit. "I think we've all done some reevaluating this past month. If he wants to offer his private plane to transport homeless animals to new homes, who am I to argue?"

Beth laughed softly. "About that flight… Look how neatly he tied in a way to see you again. Coincidence? I don't think so."

Not even having a clue how to respond to that notion, Megan clasped her daughter's hand and retreated to her office. The second she closed the door, she realized she'd done it again. Run away like the coward she'd denied being.

But when it came to Whit Daltry and the way he flipped her world with one sizzling look, keeping her cool just wasn't an option.

# Three

Whit parked his truck in the four-car garage of his large, custom-built home in Pine Valley. With a hard exhale, he slumped back in the seat. He'd spent the whole day at work thinking about seeing Megan at the shelter when he'd brought in the cat. Knowing he'd locked in a reason to see her again pumped him full of excitement. Life had sucked so badly the past month. Feeling alive again was good. Damn good.

He reached for the door and stepped out into the massive garage, all his.

Growing up, he'd lived in apartments half the size of this space, which also held a sports car, a speed boat and a motorcycle. He liked his toys and the security of knowing they were paid for. Since the day he'd left home, he'd never bought anything on credit. His college degree had been financed with a combination of scholarships and two jobs. Debt was a four-letter word to him.

His father had showered his family with gifts, but too often those presents were repossessed or abandoned as the Daltry family fled creditors yet again. His parents had passed away years ago, his dad of a stroke, his mom of a broken heart weakened from too many years of disappointment after disappointment.

Every time they'd moved to a new place, his mother wore that hopeful expression that this time would be different, that his father wouldn't gamble away the earnings from his new job, that they could stay and build a life. And every time she was wrong. Most times that hope would fade to resignation about a week before his dad announced the latest cut-and-run exit for the Daltry family. Whit came to appreciate the advance warning since it gave him the opportunity to tuck away some things before the inevitable pack-and-dash.

He'd built this house for himself as a tribute to leaving that life behind. But he'd waited to start construction. He'd refused to break ground until he had the money to pay for every square foot of it. People viewed him as lighthearted and easygoing—true enough, up to a point. No way in hell was he sinking himself into debt just to make a show of thumbing his nose at the past. He knew the pain of losing everything as a kid and he refused to go through that again. He'd been damned lucky his home in Pine Valley hadn't sustained any damage from the storm.

As he stepped from the garage into the wide passageway, he thought of all this empty space. He made a point of donating to charities, even throwing in elbow grease as well when called for, like pitching in with the never-ending cleanup after the tornado.

And now working with the animals? Except he wasn't. He'd left that cat at the shelter. He'd meant everything he said about not having time for a pet, but Megan had asked about temporary fostering and he'd rejected that out of hand. He knew he'd disappointed her with his answer. Or rather confirmed her preconceived negative notions about him.

Maybe if he got a couple of cats to keep each other company. Cats were more independent, right?

As he opened the door to the kitchen, his cell phone rang. He fished it out of his pocket and the caller ID showed…Megan Maguire?

His pulse kicked up a notch at just the sight of her name. Damn, he needed to get a grip. Pursuing her was one thing. Giving her this much control over how he felt? Not okay. He needed to keep things light, flirtatious.

He answered the phone. "Hello, pretty lady. What can I do for you?"

"Seriously?" she asked dryly. "Do you always answer the phone that way?"

"Megan?" he answered with overplayed surprise. "Well, damn, I thought it was my granny calling."

She laughed, her voice relaxing into a husky, sexy melody. "You have a granny?"

"I didn't crawl out from under a rock. I have relatives." Just really distant ones who had cut ties with his branch of the family tree long ago because of his father. "Actually, my grandmother passed away ten years ago. My cheesy line was totally for your benefit, I just didn't expect it to fall so flat. So let's start over."

That might not be a bad idea: to call for a do-over in a larger way, erase the past three and a half years.

"Sure," she said. "Hello, Whit, this is Megan Maguire. I hope I didn't disturb your supper."

"Well, hey there, Megan." He opened the stain-less-steel, oversized refrigerator and pulled out an imported beer. "What a surprise to hear from you. What do you need?"

He sat in a chair at the island where the cooking service he'd hired left a dinner in a warmer each night. He couldn't cook. Tried, but just didn't have the knack for more than grilling and he worked too late to grill. He twisted open the beer and waited for her to answer.

"I was just loading my dishwasher, and this

weird panic set in that maybe you weren't serious earlier."

"About what?" He tipped back a swig of the imported brew.

"Did you really offer your plane to transport animals?"

"Absolutely. I don't make promises I can't keep." His father was the king of broken promises, all smiles and dreams with no substance.

"Whew," she exhaled. "Thank goodness. Because I asked a contact in Colorado to check out the rescue. I also spoke with the veterinarian the rescue uses and everything appears perfect. So I called them and they can still take a dozen of our cats, a huge help to us and to local animal control. Am I being pushy in asking how soon we can transport them because I would really like to see them settled before Thanksgiving?"

"Not pushy at all." This was Thursday, with turkey day only a week away. He had a meeting he couldn't miss on Friday, but the notion of spending the weekend with her was enticing as hell. He'd hoped this would work out. He just hadn't realized how quickly the plan would come together. "Glad they have space to accommodate. I could see you're stuffed to the gills."

"Feeding and caring for so many animals is depleting our budget in a hurry." Her voice was weary, tempting him to race over to her house with his pre-cooked dinner. "We try our best to plan for disasters, but having just built the new shelter, we're stretched to the max."

He couldn't feed her tonight, but he could lighten some of her load. "I also meant it when I said I'll talk to the Cattleman's Club about rolling up their sleeves and opening their wallets. We can help. We're about more than the Stetson hats and partying."

"I honestly don't know what to say to all of this generosity. You've really come through for us with so much, especially offering your plane. Thank you."

"Glad to help. Can you have the animals ready to fly day after tomorrow? I'm free to fly them to Colorado on Saturday."

She gasped. "*You* are flying the plane? I thought you would have a pilot…."

Had he failed to mention that part of his offer?

Would she go running in the opposite direction? Not with the cats' well-being at stake. But might she try to send someone else from the shelter in her place? Had he just roped himself into a weekend with her kennel supervisor?

That didn't change his promise. He didn't break his word.

But he would definitely be disappointed to miss out on the chance to get closer to Megan.

He clicked speakerphone and placed his cell phone on the slate island. "I do have a pilot who flies me around if I need to have a meeting or entertain en-route. But I'm a licensed pilot too, quite proficient, if I do say so myself. What do you say? Let's make a weekend out of it."

"A weekend away together in Colorado?" The shock in her voice vibrated through the phone line. "Are you trying to buy your way into my life?"

"Now that stings." And oddly enough, it really did. He wanted her to think well of him. "I will concede that I'm trying to get your attention, and bringing the cat today offered an excuse to see you again, but it's not like I concocted a fake stray to meet you. Flying the other cats to Colorado is the right thing to do for the shelter and for our community. Even a hard-ass like me can see that. If you doubt my motives, bring your daughter along. She's a great kid."

The silence stretched and he checked the menu card with his meal—balsamic skirt steak with corn polenta—while he waited. Her answer was suddenly a lot more important than it should have been. But he wanted more time with her. Hell, he flat-out wanted her. He had since the first time he'd seen her. The tornado had just made him re-evaluate. Life was too short and too easily lost to put off pursuing goals.

And right now, his goal was to discover if the chemistry between him and Megan was as explosive as that one kiss led him to believe.

"So, Megan? About Saturday?" He rolled the beer bottle between both palms, anticipation firing in his gut.

"Without question, Evie would love the adventure. I'm not able to offer her much in the way of vacation or special trips. She's also been hesitant to stay at the sitter's…." Megan drew in a shaky breath. "Saturday it is then."

A thrill of victory surged through him, stronger than any he'd experienced in a damn long time.

"Excellent. And hey, feel free to make more calls and line up a place for the extra dogs and we can make it a weekly outing. Wait—before you accuse me of using the animals to get to you, the offer still stands if you want to send one of your staff in your place."

She laughed dryly. "Let's take it one week at a time."

But he knew she wouldn't be able to turn down the offer. He'd found the perfect in with her. "And by the way, a trip that long won't all fit into one day. Be sure to pack an overnight bag."

Megan held a clipboard and cross-referenced the information on the printout with the card attached to each cat carrier lined up inside Whit's aircraft. The plane could easily hold a dozen or more people, but those sofas and lounge chairs were empty. The kitty cargo had been creatively stashed beneath seats and strapped under the food station bar.

Most of the felines were already curled up and snoozing from the sedative she'd administered prior to crating them. Three of the cats, though, were staring back at her with wide, drugged eyes and the occasional hiss, hanging on to consciousness and looking at her suspiciously. Sheba, an all-black fluff ball, had come from a home where she was an only pet and queen of her domain, but after her owner passed away, the extended family had dumped their mother's beloved pet at the shelter. Sheba had been freaked out and terrified ever since. She needed a home environment, even a foster setting, until an adopter could be found. Skittles, an orange tabby stray, had been found at the shopping mall with no name tag, no microchip and no one to claim her. If she went much longer without a home setting, Megan feared Skittles would turn feral. And the third of the cranky passengers, Sebastian, was a gorgeous, very huge Maine Coon cat that desperately needed more space to move around than the shelter could offer.

Provided the Colorado group was as wonderful in person as her contact and the vet indicated, by evening the twelve cats would be with a rescue that only operated with foster homes until adoptive homes were found. No more shelter life for them.

She rested a hand on top of a crate, exhaustion from the past month seeping through her. Maybe now that she had some help in sight, her body was finally relaxing enough to let all those extra hours catch up with her. She still could hardly believe this was happening—and thanks to Whit Daltry, of all people. The last man she would have expected to go the extra mile for her.

But the very man who'd done more than that for her when he'd helped her reach Evie after the tornado.

Megan stole a quick glance to check on her daughter, currently sprawled out asleep on one of the leather sofas. They'd had to get up early to ready the cats at the shelter. Evie had insisted on wearing a cowgirl outfit today—with the ever present tiara, of course.

Footsteps sounded outside on the metal stairs,

and a second later Whit filled the hatch. He looked Texas-awesome, with broad shoulders—as if Texas ever did anything half way. He wore a chambray button-down with the sleeves rolled up. And his jeans—Lord help her. The well-washed denim fit him just right. Her mouth watered. He ducked and pulled off his hat to clear the hatch on his way inside.

"Everything's a go outside whenever you and Evie are ready to buckle in." His boots thudded against the carpeted floor as he walked to Megan and rested a hand on her shoulder.

Static sparked through her so tangibly she could almost believe crackles filled and lit the air. Whit's clean soap scent brought to mind the image of a shared morning shower, a notion far too intimate to entertain, especially when they had to spend the next two days in close confines. She eased away from him under the guise of flipping the page on her clipboard. Except it was already the last page so she looked too obvious.

Quickly, she flipped all the papers back into place.

Whit stuffed his hands in his jean pockets. "We might as well talk about it."

"Talk about what?" How she couldn't peel her eyes off his strong jaw? Could barely suppress the urge to step closer and brush her cheek along the fresh-shaven texture of his face? She was having a hard time remembering why she had to stay away from this man.

"When you kissed me."

"Shhhh!" she whispered urgently. "Do you want someone—Evie—to hear?" Her daughter was a great big reason she needed to tread warily with any man she let into their lives.

He stepped closer. "Okay, how's this?"

His voice rumbled over her like the vibration of quiet thunder in a summer rain. Desire pooled low in her belly, her breasts tingling and tightening as if the first drops of that summer storm were caressing her bare skin.

Damn. She was in deep trouble here.

She clutched the clipboard to her chest. "I didn't kiss you that day. Not exactly."

"I remember the day well. Your lips on mine. That's a kiss," he bantered with a devilish glint in his eyes. "But just so that we're clear, none of this trip today is contingent on there being another kiss."

"I meant to kiss your cheek as…a thanks." A mind-melting, toe-curling thanks. "You're the one who turned your face and made it into something more."

He dipped his head and spoke softly, his breath warm against her ear. "And you're the one who smells like cinnamon and has this sexy kitten moan. I dream of hearing it again."

She fought back the urge to moan at just the sound of his voice and the memories his words evoked. "I thought you were taking the animals on this flight as a totally philanthropic act."

"I am."

She tipped her chin and stood her ground. "Then what's this flirting about?"

"I'm a multitasker." He knocked on the clipboard still clasped against her breasts. "Let's get strapped in and ready to roll."

An hour later, Megan rested her arm along the sofa back and watched the puffy white clouds filling the sky. The plane cruised as smoothly as if they were cushioned by those pillowy clouds, not a bump yet to disconcert her.

Shortly after takeoff, Evie had asked to join Whit. Megan had started to say no, but apparently he'd heard and waved her daughter up front to the empty co-pilot's seat. As a single parent, Megan was so used to being the sole caregiver and primary form of entertainment for her daughter—especially since the tornado. This moment to relax with her thoughts was a welcome reprieve.

Hell, to relax at all seemed like a gift.

The cats were all happily snoozing now in their tranquilized haze. No more evil eye from the three stubborn ones that had stayed awake the longest.

Her gaze shifted back to her daughter up front. Evie, rejuvenated from her nap, was now chattering to Whit. He sat at the helm, piloting them through the skies with obvious ease and skill. His hands and feet moved in perfect synch, his eyes scanning the control as he seamlessly carried on a convoluted conversation with her four-year-old daughter.

"Mr. Whit, I'm a cowgirl," Evie declared proudly.

"I see that," he answered patiently as if she hadn't already been peppering his ear with accounts of every detail of her life from her best friends at school—Caitlyn and Bobby—to what she ate for breakfast this morning—a granola bar and chocolate milk in the car on the way to the shelter. "Last week, you were a knight with a sword."

"A princess knight," she said as if he was too slow to have noticed the difference.

Megan suppressed a smile.

"Right," Whit answered. "You always wear that pretty tiara."

"This week, I'm keeping the monsters away with my rope." She patted her hip where the miniature lasso was hooked to her belt loop. "It's a lassie."

"Lassie? Oh, lasso. I see," he said solemnly. "You're going to rope the monsters?"

Megan swallowed down a lump of emotion at how easily he saw through to her daughter's fears.

"Yep, sir, that's right," Evie answered with a nod that threatened to dislodge her tiara. "Rope 'em up and throw 'em in the trash."

He stayed silent for a heart-stopping second before he answered with a measured calm, "You're a very brave little girl."

Evie shrugged. "Somebody's gotta do it."

Megan choked back a bittersweet laugh as her daughter parroted one of her mommy's favorite phrases.

Whit glanced at Evie. "Your mommy takes very good care of you. You're safe now, kiddo."

"But nobody takes care of Mommy. That's not fair."

Megan blinked back tears at the weight her little girl was carrying around inside. He didn't seem to have a ready answer to that one. Neither did Megan.

Evie hitched up her feet to sit cross-legged, picking at the Velcro of her new tennis shoes. They hadn't been able to afford cowgirl boots, not with new shoes to buy. "I'm not sure what I'll be next. Gotta look through my costume box and see what'll scare the monsters."

"Where are these monsters?"

"They come out of the sky with the wind." Evie pointed ahead at the windscreen and made swirly gestures with her spindly, little-girl arms. "So I'm riding wif you in the plane. I'll get 'em before they scare other kids."

Megan tipped her head back to hold in the tears. She had seen this flight as a welcome distraction for her child. She hadn't considered Evie might be afraid, and certainly not for this particular reason. But it made perfect sense, and somehow Whit had gotten more information on the fears in one simple conversation than Megan had been able to pry out of her strong-willed child in the past month.

Evie wiggled her feet. "I got new shoes. They light up when I walk."

"Very nice."

"My princess sneakers got messed up in the tora-na-do." She pronounced the word much better these days than a month ago.

They'd all had lots of practice with the word.

Whit glanced at Evie for an instant, his brown

eyes serious and compassionate. "I'm so sorry to hear that."

"They were my favorites. But we couldn't find ones just like 'em. I think these lights are a good idea. I coulda used the lights the day the tora-na-do made the school all dark."

Megan's stomach plummeted as surely as if the plane had lost serious altitude. Was every choice her child made tied into that day now? Megan had thought the shoe-shopping trip had been a fun day for Evie, and yet the whole time her daughter had assessed every choice using survivalist criteria. Megan blinked back tears and focused on listening to Evie.

"Mommy says lots of little girls lost their shoes too and we need to be glad we gots shoes."

"Your mother is a smart lady."

Was it her imagination or had he just glanced back at her out of the corner of his eye? A shiver of awareness tingled up her spine.

"I know, and I wanna be good like Mommy so Santa will come visit my house."

His head tipped to the side inquisitively. "Santa

will see what a very good girl you've been today. I suspect you're always a good girl."

"Not as good as Mommy."

Megan frowned in surprise, her heart aching all over again for what her daughter had been through and how little Evie had shared about that. Until now. Somehow Whit had a way of reaching her that no one else had. Megan was grateful, and nervous to think of him gaining more importance in her life.

Whit waited a moment before answering, "Why do you think that about yourself, kiddo?"

Evie just shook her head, pigtails swishing and tiara landing in her lap. "Let's talk about something else. Caitlyn and Bobby are my bestest friends. Are you Mommy's new bestest friend?"

# Four

As the sun set at the end of a chilly day, Whit cranked the heat inside the rental car, an SUV that had been perfect for transporting the twelve cats to their new foster families with the Colorado rescue group. They'd just finished their last drop-off. Mission complete.

Megan had insisted on inspecting every home in spite of the long day and the Colorado cold. But in the end, she was satisfied she'd found a great new rescue to network with in the future.

Glancing at the rearview mirror, Whit watched Megan strapped her daughter into the car seat, a task he'd learned she never allowed anyone else to take over no matter how many stops they made. Evie had been patient, excited even, over seeing her mom in action. And the couple of times the kid had gotten bored, she'd been easily distracted by the snow flurries—which had necessitated a side trip to pick up a warmer snow suit and snow boots.

Evie had been hesitant about covering her costume and her trepidation stabbed Whit clean through with sympathy for the little tyke. Finally, he'd been able to persuade her even cowgirls needed cold weather gear more appropriate for Colorado—which was a helluva lot colder than Texas.

Megan tucked into the passenger side as they idled outside a two-story farmhouse belonging to an older widower inside who'd made a fuss over his feline visitor. She rubbed her gloved hands together in front of the heat vent and then swiped the snowflakes off her head.

"I miss Texas," she said between her chattering teeth. "If you ever hear me complain during the winter, just remind me of this day."

That implied they would keep in contact after

this weekend. He was making progress in comparison to their previous standoff. Did this mean she'd forgiven him for claiming the land she'd wanted for the shelter? He wasn't going to push his luck by asking. He intended to ride the wave of her good mood today and build some more positive memories.

Megan deserved to have some fun and recreation.

He'd seen firsthand how she carried a ton of worries around for one person, between taking care of her daughter alone and spreading her generous heart even thinner for these homeless animals. Who looked after Megan? Who gave her a break from life's burdens?

He turned his heater vents in her direction as well. "You accomplished a lot in one day."

"It's a relief to have them settled, and so quickly." She reached back to Evie and squeezed her daughter's hand. "Did you have fun?"

"I like the plane and the snow." She kicked her feet. "And my new boots that Mr. Whit bought me."

"Good, I'm glad, sweetie. We'll get a Happy

Meal before going back to the…hotel." She swallowed, her eyes darting nervously to Whit. "Thank you again for arranging everything."

He put the SUV into drive and pulled out onto the tree-lined suburban road, leaving the last foster home behind. "What about other rescues? Did you find more places that can help out with some of the animals back home?"

Her green eyes lit with excitement. "I have a line on a couple of breed-specific rescues that might be able to take a few of our beagles and our German Shepherd." She touched his arm lightly; it was the first physical contact she'd initiated since that kiss. "But I can't keep asking you to take off work to fly around the country."

"I have a private pilot and I'm guessing if you already know the reputation of the rescue, then the animals can fly alone with him." While the obvious answer would be to lock in their weekends with more of these flights together, he also knew a more subtle approach would win Megan over. Just as he'd told Evie, her mama was smart and Whit was drawn to that part of Megan as well. So he opted for a smoother approach. "This doesn't always have to be about us spending time together. Not that I'm complaining. What? You look surprised."

He bit back a self-satisfied smile and steered out onto the rural mountain road into a smattering of five o'clock traffic.

She tipped her head to the side, the setting sun casting a warm glow over her face. "You would pay your pilot to fly just one or two dogs at a time?"

"Sure, although I've also got an idea for recruiting some of my friends to help out." He accelerated past a slow-moving vehicle backing up traffic. "A number of them own planes, short range, long range, and we all like to pitch in and help. Sometimes we just need pointing in the right direction."

"Even if you don't get to see me and make moves to follow up on…." She glanced up at the rearview mirror and watched Evie playing with her iPad. "Even if you know there won't be a replay of what happened a month ago."

"I can separate work and personal, just as I can separate personal and philanthropic. And," he ducked his head closer to hers, "I can also blend them when the situation presents itself. Like today."

Evie kicked the back of her mother's seat. "Can I have my Happy Meal, please? 'Cause if I have to wait much longer, I'm gonna starve and then it would be a Sad Meal."

Whit choked on a laugh. God, this kid was a cute little imp. "Absolutely, kiddo, we can get supper for you. And then after supper, I have plans."

Megan sat up straighter. "Plans?"

Damn straight. He had an agenda full of fun for a woman who didn't get much in the way of recreation. "Unless you have an objection, we'll have dinner and ice skating before we turn in for the night."

Ice skating.

Megan never would have guessed the mega-wealthy, smooth operator Whit Daltry would plan a night of ice skating and burgers. Granted, they were the best burgers she'd ever eaten. But still, the laid-back quality of fun appealed to her.

He'd also taken Evie into account, something else that set him apart from other men who'd asked her out for a date—except wait, this wasn't a date. She didn't have time for dating.

Right?

She sat on a bench by the outdoor skating rink, eating the last of her sweet potato fries and watching Whit lead her daughter carefully as she found her balance on the children's skates. Moonbeams and halogen lights created the effect of a hazy dome over the crowded ice, which was full of people getting into the Christmas spirit early. His patience was commendable. A person couldn't fake that. He genuinely had a knack with kids.

Megan could see her daughter's mouth moving non-stop as she chattered away, her breath puffing clouds in tiny bursts. Whit nodded periodically. Other skaters whipped past, but he kept up the slow, steady pace with Evie, making sure to keep her safe.

She stopped and tugged his hand, so cute in her puffy pink snowsuit next to Whit, who towered over her in his blue parka. He knelt, listening intently. Then he stood, scooping her up and skating faster, faster, faster still. Evie's squeals of delight carried on the wind, mixing with music piping through the outdoor sound system. Megan's heart softened, a dangerous emotion because this could be so easy to get used to, to depend on. To crave.

*Him.*

She exhaled a very long stream of white vapor. She needed to steel herself and tread warily. She ate three sweet potato fries. Fast. Feeding her stomach because she couldn't address the deeper hunger.

Whit and her daughter circled the rink twice before he skidded to a stop in front of Megan's bench. He held Evie confidently. Her cheeks were pink from the cold, her little girl's smile wide and genuine for the first time since the twister tore apart their lives.

Megan scooted over on the bench to make room for them to join her. She patted the chilly metal with her gloved hand. "You're very good at ice skating for a Texan."

Whit lowered Evie to sit between them. "My parents moved around a lot when I was growing up, all over the U.S., actually. I spent some time ice skating on ponds because we couldn't afford the admission to a rink."

That explained why his accent wasn't as strong as others who lived in Royal. But she'd assumed he still came from a privileged background because he fit so seamlessly into the elite Texas world typified by the TCC members. She tried to picture him as a kid fitting in at all those new places. He'd earned all that confidence the hard way. She understood that road well.

"What other skills did you pick up over the years?" Megan passed her daughter the box of fries.

"You'll have to wait to find out." He stretched his arm along the back of the bench and tugged a curly lock of her hair.

"A man of mystery." Had she actually leaned into his touch? The warmth of his arm seared her through her coat and sweater and the temptation to stay right here burned strong.

"Just trying to keep you around."

Evie dropped her fry and looked up with worried green eyes. "Where's Mommy going?"

"Nowhere, sweetie." She gathered her child close to her side, love and the deep importance of her role as Evie's mom twining inside her. "I'm staying with you."

Her daughter continued to stare up at her. "Are you sure?"

"Absolutely."

Evie looked down at her ice skates, chewing her lip before turning to Whit. "You said I could pick somethin' from the gift shop."

Megan gasped, ducking her head to meet her daughter's eyes. "Evie! You shouldn't ask Mr. Daltry to buy you things. He's already been very generous with this trip for the kitties and then entertaining us with ice skating."

He squeezed Megan's shoulder. "It's okay. Evie's right. I offered, downright promised. And a person should always do their best to keep their promises."

Megan raised her gloved hands in surrender. "Sounds like I'm outvoted."

"Yay!" Evie giggled.

Whit hefted her up, keeping his balance on the ice skates. "Did you have something already picked out, kiddo?"

She bobbed her head, pigtails swinging around her earmuffs—which she had instead of a hat so she could still wear her tiara. "I wanna get the snow princess costume so I can freeze the monsters."

Megan's stomach plummeted. This night may have felt like a magical escape from real life. But she couldn't afford to forget for a second that her everyday reality and responsibilities were still waiting for her once this fantasy weekend was over.

This night was all she could have with Whit.

The more time he spent with Megan on this trip, the more Whit was certain he should take his time with her, get to know her. Win her over gradually once they got home.

For now, here in their cozy ski chalet, he needed to keep his distance. He needed to bide his time. Rushing her tonight could well cost him all the progress he'd made. Megan wasn't the type to be interested in a one-night stand, and quite frankly, he couldn't imagine that once with her would be enough.

The chalet was a three-bedroom in Vail, with a full sitting room and kitchen that overlooked a lake. He'd originally gotten three bedrooms to assure Megan that he respected her privacy, while still leaving their options open. But that timetable had changed.

He'd just finished building a fire in the old-fashioned fireplace when Evie's bedroom door opened and Megan stepped out. Her hair was loose and curlier than normal around her face after their evening at the windy ice rink. She still wore her jeans and green fuzzy sweater, no shoes though, just thick socks. Her toes wiggled into the carpet as if she was anchoring herself in the room. Finally, he had her alone and today of all days he'd resolved to bide his time.

It would take all his restraint to keep himself in check.

Tucking aside some extra logs to keep the fire burning for a few more hours, he stepped behind the wet bar and pulled out a bottle of sparkling water. "Would you like something to drink? The bar is stocked. There's juice and some herbal tea…"

"Any wine? Preferably red." She slid a band off her wrist and tugged her hair back to gather it into a low ponytail. "One glass won't incapacitate me."

"Oh, sure," he said, surprised. He scanned the selection and found a good bottle from a reputable California vineyard. He poured a glass for her, water for himself. He passed her the crystal glass.

She savored a sip and smiled, sinking down in the middle of a pile of throw pillows on the sofa. She could have chosen the chair, but she'd left room for him to sit, even sweeping aside one of the pillows to clear a space. Intentional or not? He kept his silence and waited while she gazed into the fire for a long moment.

"Thank you for everything, Whit. For bringing us here, for going to so much trouble to arrange such a special evening for Evie too." Megan tucked her legs to the side, the flames from the fire casting a warm glow on her skin. "It was an incredible way to end an already wonderful day."

As she shifted, her socks scrunched down to

her ankles, revealing a tiny paw print tattoo. How had he never noticed that before? Did she have others hidden elsewhere on her body? His gaze fixed on that mark for an instant before he took his tumbler and sat in the leather chair beside her.

Was that a flicker of disappointment in her eyes?

"No trouble at all," he said. "This has been a nice change of pace from eating alone or playing darts at the club."

"You aren't fooling me for a second." Her green eyes twinkled with mischief. "Your life is much more fast-paced than that."

"If you're asking if I'm seeing anyone, the answer is no." Although the fact that she would ask gave him hope he was on the right track playing this cool, taking his time. "You have my complete and undivided attention."

Her eyes went wide and she chewed her bottom lip. "Really?"

He angled back, hitching a booted foot on his knee. "That was impressive seeing you in action today. You were amazing interviewing the foster families and sifting through all that paperwork. I had no idea how much detail went into ensuring the animals are safe and well cared for."

"I'm just doing my job, a job I'm very happy to have. I get to do the work I love in an environment that is flexible about letting my daughter join me. It's the best of both worlds and I intend to be worthy of keeping the position."

"Well, I don't know a lot about the animal rescue world, but from what I can tell, whatever they're paying you can't be nearly enough for how much heart you pour into saving each one of those cats and dogs."

"We're all called to make a difference in the world. This is my way," she said simply and sipped her wine, her eyes tracking him with a hint of confusion.

*Keep on course.*

And he found himself actually wanting to get to know her better. Staying in the chair and finding out more about Megan wasn't such a hardship. "What made you choose this line of work?"

"I've always loved animals."

"But it must be more than that."

She eyed him over the rim of her glass. "Most people accept the simple answer."

"I'm not most people."

He stared back, waiting even though he wanted to close the space between them and lay her down along that sofa. He burned to cover her, kiss her. Take her.

"Well, while other girls were reading *Little House on the Prairie* or Nancy Drew novels, I devoured everything I could find on animals, their history, how to care for them, how to train them." The more she spoke, the more she relaxed on the throw pillows piled on the corner of the sofa. "I had these dreams of going to the big dog shows with my pup Snickers. I watched the shows over and over again so I could train him to do all the moves."

She was so buttoned up and proper, all about the rules, he hadn't expected such a quirky story from her. He wanted to know more. "What happened?"

Megan rolled her eyes and lifted her glass in toast. "Somehow I missed the memo that the dog show was just for purebreds."

"What kind of dog did you have?"

"A Jack Russell-Shih Tzu mix. Absolutely adorable and somehow unacceptable." She shook her head. "Wrong."

"I'm sorry you didn't get to have your big show with that pup."

Her gaze narrowed to a steely determination he'd seen before, except he'd been the cause of her ire then.

"Oh, I made sure Snickers still had his moment in the sun. I trained him to ride a skateboard, made a video and sent it into the *Late Night* show. Imagine my mom's surprise when they contacted us. I went on the show. And my dog was famous for a week."

He leaned back with a chuckle of admiration. "If you did that today, you'd get a reality show."

"You could be right."

"You were famous for more than a week. I remember that story now...."

"I ran the talk show circuit until my fifteen minutes of fame was up."

He blinked in surprise. "Somehow I didn't guess you were a limelight seeker. I envisioned you more as the studious type, the crusader in a more conventional way. Now I see where Evie gets her showmanship."

She laughed. "We've never really spent enough time with each other to form opinions."

"You must have been fearless." His mind filled with images of her as a child, as quirky and incredible as little Evie. "Most kids would be scared to put themselves in front of the camera that would broadcast them to the whole world."

"I was hoping my father would see me." She sipped her wine and stared into the flames crackling in the fireplace.

"Your dad?" he prompted.

"My biological father wasn't in my life. He made child support payments and sent a birthday card with a check each year, which puts him one step ahead of Evie's dad, who hasn't so much as bought her a pair of shoes." She cleared her throat. "But back to my father. I know he saw the show because he mentioned it in my next birthday card. He'd noticed, but it didn't change a thing." She shrugged. "I found out later he was married. I worry about Evie, since her father's chosen not to be a part of her life."

"I imagine it doesn't help to hear that missing even a minute with Evie is his loss."

She held up a hand. "Stop, I don't want sympathy. I love my daughter and I've worked hard to build this life. I just want her to have an easier path, to find a man who will value what a gift she is."

"That makes sense."

She leaned forward, elbows on the arm rest. "I'm not sure you're hearing me though. I can't afford to make another mistake in a relationship. I have to be a good example as her mother, as a woman."

Was she tossing him on his ass before they even got started? He angled forward, and suddenly the space between them wasn't so great after all. "That doesn't mean you can't have a social life."

"I need to be careful for my daughter." She nibbled on her bottom lip. "So things like dating, especially now, need to be on hold."

She half rose from the sofa and her mouth was a mere inch away from his as he sat in the leather chair beside her. Her pupils widened with unmistakable arousal. But she'd just said she wasn't interested in dating. He had to be misreading her… unless…she wanted a one-night stand, which was ironic as hell since she was the first woman he'd had serious thoughts about dating in a very long time. Before he could wrap his brain around that thought—

She kissed him.

# Five

Shimmers of desire tingled through her.

Megan settled her mouth against his. It was no impulsive "thank you" this time. She'd thought it out, planning to make the most of this evening with Whit. She could indulge in this much before returning to everyday life and responsibilities.

She'd spent so much of the past three and a half years annoyed at Whit, resisting the attraction. Until now. She'd been tempted, seeing the altruistic side of him that she'd heard about but he'd done his best to keep hidden from her. Then watching him with her daughter totally slayed her.

Just one night. That's all she could have. And she intended to make the most of it.

Her lips parted against his, encouraging… *Yes.* His tongue traced along her mouth, sweeping inside to meet hers. Kissing. She'd longed for a man's kiss, the bold give and take, the hard planes of a masculine body.

Of his body.

Whit.

She'd been attracted to him from the start, and resented those feelings since they'd been at odds over the property dispute. Not to mention he wasn't particularly known for being environ-mental friendly. She'd given him an earful once over his purchase of a piece of wetlands.

However, even if they hadn't been adversar-ies, she'd been wary of dating because of her lit-tle girl, who was less than a year old then. The memory of Evie's father's betrayal had still been so fresh. She'd been struggling to put her life together and Whit had threatened to rock that. She'd been tempted though, then deeply disap-pointed when he quickly squelched those fanta-sies by being a ruthless land baron, causing her constant headaches.

The ache was lower now, pooling between her legs.

She thrust her fingers into his hair, and something seemed to snap inside of him. His muscular arms wrapped around her, hauling her closer until her chest pressed to his and she sat on his lap. She wriggled against him and straddled his legs, kneeling on the leather chair. His low growl of approval rumbled against her, flaming the heat inside her higher, hotter.

His hands slid down her back in a steady caress to cup her hips. The steady press of his fingers carefully sinking into her flesh had her writhing closer. It had been so long since she'd languished in these sensations of total, lush arousal. Maybe she was feeling emotional in the wake of the storm's destruction, leading her to want something more.

And judging from his response, he felt the same. She'd known he was attracted to her too. She couldn't miss that in his eyes. But feeling the thick length of his arousal against her stomach sent her senses reeling.

His mouth moved along her jaw, then down her

neck, his breath caressing along her overheated skin. Her head fell back to give him better access and with each breath she drew in the scent of his aftershave mixed with the sweet smell of fragrant smoke wafting up from the fireplace.

He stroked her arms, then ran his hands up over her shoulders to cup her face. The snag of his callused fingertips sent a thrill through her. He was a man of infinite finesse and raspy masculinity all at once. Would they go to her bedroom or his? She had condoms in her purse. Always. She loved her daughter but she wouldn't risk an unplanned pregnancy.

The thought threatened to chill her and she sealed her mouth to Whit's again, her fingers crawling under his sweater to explore the solid wall of his chest. His touch trailed back down her arms in a delicious sweep until he clasped her wrists.

And pulled her hands away from him.

She blinked in confusion. "Whit?"

He angled back, his brown eyes almost black with emotion. "You're beautiful. I've fantasized about what your hair feels like so many times."

Then he cradled her hips in his palms again and shifted her off his lap and onto the sofa. Were they going to take things further out here? She opened her mouth to suggest they go to her room when she realized he wasn't sitting down again.

She reached up for him, ready to follow him wherever. He took her hand and pressed a kiss to her palm.

His eyes held hers. "Thanks for an amazing day. I look forward to tomorrow." He squeezed her hand once before letting go. "Goodnight, Megan. See you in the morning."

Cool air chilled over her flaming face. The first time she'd kissed him she could write off as an accident and save her pride. But not now. And he'd clearly been turned on and into the moment. So why the rejection?

Damn it all, she didn't have time in her life for games. Anger took root inside her, fueled by frustrated desire. As far as she was concerned, he could take his mixed signals and stuff them.

She would communicate with him on a professional level for the animals. But beyond that, she was done throwing herself at Whit Daltry.

* * *

As Whit landed his plane on the runway back in Royal, he couldn't help but compare this journey home to their flight out to Colorado. Yesterday's trip had been full of chatter and fun. The whole day had been one of the best he could remember. And he wanted more of them—with Megan and with Evie. Which meant he had to stay the course. As much as he'd wanted to follow through on Megan's invitation last night, he sensed she wasn't as ready as her kiss indicated.

So today, he sat up front alone at the plane's helm, while Evie stayed in the back napping beside her mom. The craft glided along the runway, slowing, slowing, slowing. He taxied up to the small airport that serviced their little town, the only place that had ever felt like home.

Megan had stayed quiet all day for the most part, giving only one or two answers to his questions about her work. Had he offended her last night? He'd only intended to ramp her interest, to take his time rather than rush her and risk her bolting. And now she'd bolted anyway after one of the most explosive kisses of his life. Only a kiss, damn it.

A cinnamon-scented moment.

The memory of that instant with her had him hard and wanting her now. But from the steely set of her jaw and straight spine, another kiss wasn't welcome. He had some serious backpedaling to do.

He steered the plane into the appointed parking spot. His employees converged outside to service the plane, unload the luggage and all the empty animal crates. He opened the hatch and lowered the steps while Megan unbuckled her napping daughter. Megan hefted Evie up into her arms and paused by Whit, her eyes scrubbed free of any emotion.

"Thank you for everything," she said with a careful smile.

He touched her elbow. "It was a good weekend."

"I should get home to relieve the pet sitter. Evie and I need to tackle washing before Monday hits." She nibbled her bottom lip, anger flickering in her eyes.

Well, hell. That cleared up any questions. He didn't have to wonder if he'd upset her by giving her time and space. And in the process, he'd denied them both an incredible night together for no reason at all. He needed to let her know he wasn't rejecting her, just…giving her time to adjust to the change in their relationship. "Do you need help with anything? I'll have the crates delivered back to the shelter."

"Thank you," she said tightly, then looked away for a second, adjusting her hold on her daughter before meeting his gaze head-on again. "Listen, about last night when I kissed you—"

He tapped her lips. "Would you like to spend Thanksgiving together?"

Her eyes went wide with shock. "What?"

"Let's spend Thanksgiving together." He hadn't planned on that particular offer, per se, but it made perfect sense now as a way to show her he was serious. "Last night wasn't a game to me. Your place or mine, whichever you want. I don't expect you to cook for me."

"What is going on with you? You're giving me

whiplash." She cupped Evie's head. "You plan to make the meal?" She laughed skeptically.

"If you don't mind ptomaine poisoning." He scratched the back of his neck. "Actually, I have a cooking service and they'll cater Thanksgiving. Unless I got a better offer from you and Evie."

"No." She shook her head without hesitation. "I'm sorry. But no. Spending the holiday together would give Evie the false expectations about the two of us."

She was turning him down?

Okay, now he was truly confused. "We just spent the weekend together. How is an afternoon of turkey a problem?"

"You didn't hear me. It's Thanksgiving. A holiday. That's for families." Her throat bobbed with a quick swallow. "Last night, I, uh, I didn't mean to give you the wrong impression with that kiss."

"What impression was I supposed to get?" He braced a hand on the open doorway, trying to get a read on her. She'd kissed him, made it clear she was ready for sex but didn't want anything—

close. Damn. She'd wanted a quickie with him and nothing more.

Now he was mad.

"Whit, you don't have to worry about me throwing myself at you anymore."

"Seriously?" he said, unable to believe he'd so misread this woman. "You expect us to go back to avoiding each other after the weekend we just spent together?"

"Not at all. I can behave maturely as I trust you can too. We both have to live in this town." Without another word, she descended the stairs and stepped out into the sunshine. The rays streamed over her hair, turning it into a beacon, and he couldn't peel his eyes away.

Damn, she was hot when she was all fired up. Of course she was hot any time. And while he'd misjudged her intent with the kiss Saturday, he hadn't misread her interest. For some reason she thought a one-night stand would suffice, but she was wrong.

He would give her some space for now. Holidays were tough. He got that. But after Thanksgiving?

They would not be ignoring each other.

* * *

Monday morning, Megan carried her sleepy daughter with her into work. The familiar chorus of barking dogs greeted her, reminding her of her responsibilities here, to all of the animals still in need of homes. Saturday's placement of twelve cats had been an amazing coup for such a small shelter. She couldn't afford to turn down Whit's generous offer of his plane, but she also couldn't put her heart at risk again.

The weekend with Whit had been better than she could have dreamed. He'd been charming, helpful, generous. He'd been amazing with her daughter.

And he'd been a perfect gentleman.

She was the one who'd gone off the rails and kissed him. She'd literally thrown herself at him. Again. Sure, he'd responded, but then he'd pulled away. She was starting to feel silly.

Except she knew she hadn't misread the signs. He wanted her too. So why did he keep pulling away? She'd all but promised him a night of no-strings sex and he'd still walked.

Usually guys bailed out because she had a kid.

Those guys were easy to spot. They were awkward with Evie. But Whit wasn't that way.

Had he freaked out that there was a child in the picture at the last minute anyway? She didn't think so. His eyes had still smoked over her at every turn Sunday. But she hadn't felt up to the embarrassment of doing a postmortem on how he'd walked away from taking that kiss to its natural conclusion.

Damn it, she didn't have time for these kinds of games in her life. Which was the very reason she'd wanted one night, just one night with him.

She nodded to Beth at the front desk and walked past to settle Evie in her office on the small sofa. Evie had chosen a doctor's costume today, to cure all the people and animals hurt in the tornado. The post-Halloween sales had filled Evie's costume box to overflowing. Every time Megan or one of her friends offered to buy her a toy, Evie shook her head and picked another outfit. Megan had thought about counseling, even discussed it with the preschool director. Sue Ellen had pointed her in the direction of some videos the other children in the preschool had watched together, but so far those hadn't effected any changes in Evie.

Megan sagged against the open door frame.t

Beth waved from the desk. "Good morning. How was your weekend?"

She dodged the question that she didn't even really know how to answer. "You're here early."

Beth cradled a mug of herbal tea, the scent of oranges and spices drifting across the room. "The kennel supervisor let me in. I wanted to see your face when you came to the shelter today."

Alarms sounded in Megan's mind. "Is something wrong?"

"Things are very right." Beth set aside her mug. "A dozen guys—and women—from the Cattleman's Club spent the weekend volunteering."

Another reason to be grateful to a man she'd spent the past three and half years resenting. "Whit said he intended to ask them to help out…."

And she was grateful. She'd assumed a couple of them would come by to play with the dogs.

"Well, they did more than help out. In addition to doing the regular cleaning and exercising the dogs, they fixed the broken kennel run and cleared an area behind the play yard that's been full of debris. They said they'll be back after Thanksgiving weekend to build an agility course for the dogs and add a climbing tree for the cat house." Beth winked, her eyes twinkling with mischief. "You must have really impressed him."

Megan's knees felt wobbly. He'd coordinated all that effort this weekend while she'd been thinking about a quick fling? She'd had Whit Daltry all wrong. All. Wrong.

"Whit mentioned putting in a call, but I had no idea how much they would do. Especially when everyone is still dealing with the upheaval in their own lives."

"They care about each other and our community. They just needed pointing in this direction to help. It's okay to ask for help every now and again, Megan. You don't have to be a superwoman."

She nodded tightly. "For the animals, absolutely."

"For yourself."

Megan stayed silent, uncomfortable with the direction of the conversation. She was happy with her life, damn it. She was looking forward to spending Thanksgiving with her daughter, eating turkey nuggets and sweet potato fries.

Memories of Evie's laughter at the ice skating rink taunted her with all she might be missing.

"So?" Beth tipped back the office chair and sipped her tea. "How did things go with you and Whit on the great kitty transport?"

"Fantastic. The rescue is all foster-home-based, so every cat is now placed with a family until an adopter is found." Megan opted for impersonal facts. She walked to the shelves by a small table and straightened adoption applications and promotional flyers. After Thanksgiving, she would need to put up a small Santa Paws tree for donations. So much to do. She didn't have time for anything else. "I even made some notes for our shelter on how they handle their foster system."

"Sounds like Whit is really bending over backwards to mend fences with you."

Megan crossed her arms over her chest that still yearned for the press of Whit's body against hers. "As you said, we all need to do what's best for the community right now."

"Sure, and sometimes it's personal." Standing, Beth said, gently, "Like now."

"I never even implied—"

"You don't have to. You're blushing!" Beth pointed, her nails short and neat. She stepped closer and whispered, "What happened while you were in Colorado? Come on. I tell you everything. Spill!"

"There's nothing to tell." Sadly. Megan had wanted more and still didn't know why he'd pulled away. "My daughter was with me. How about we discuss your love life? Yours definitely has more traction than mine. How are things with you and Drew Farrell? Have you set a date?"

"Weeellll, a Valentine's wedding would be nice, but we'll see." She set aside her mug with a contented sigh. "For now, we're enjoying being together and in love. Repairs are still going on at my house. Once they're done, we'll decide if I'm going to sell or stay at Drew's."

"How's Stormy?"

Beth had adopted a cocker spaniel mix from

the shelter, similar to her dog Gus that had died. Stormy had stolen Beth's heart when she'd volunteered after the tornado. "Full of mischief and a total delight."

"And the cats?" She stalled for time.

When Drew first dropped Beth off at the shelter after the storm to help Megan with cleanup, Megan encouraged Drew to take a couple of cats home with him. He'd insisted he was allergic to cats, but Megan could tell he and Beth were both enchanted. Since the kittens had come from a feral litter, placing them would have proved difficult at a time when they were already packed. Megan had mentioned the possibility of him needing barn cats—and it was a match made in heaven.

"They spend more time indoors than in the barn. Drew pops a couple of antihistamines and watches ball games with them in his lap." Home-and-hearth bliss radiated from her smile. "It's adorable."

Megan didn't begrudge Beth that joy, but God, it stung today of all days. "I'm happy for you both. For Stormy and the cats too. Thank you for taking them."

"Our pleasure."

Hearing how easily Beth said "our," Megan couldn't help but ask, "You and Drew were enemies for so long. How did you overcome that negative history so easily?"

"Who said it was easy?"

"Oh, but—"

Beth rested a hand on hers. "It's worth the effort." She sat back with a sigh. "I'm still in the 'pinch me' stage with this relationship. It's everything I didn't dare to dream of growing up."

Beth was a jeans-and-cotton-shirts kind of girl, with a causal elegance she didn't seem to realize she had. If anything, she was a little insecure in spite of all her success, sensitive about her past and the whole notion of having grown up on the wrong side of the tracks.

Megan gave Beth an impulsive hug. "It's real." She leaned back with a smile. "I've seen the way he looks at you and I'm so happy for you, my friend."

"Thank you." Beth hugged Megan back. "By

the way, I noticed you dodged answering my question about Whit. I only ask because I care. I want you to be happy. You deserve to have more in your life than work."

"I have my daughter." Megan sat at the table set up for people to fill out adoption applications, the Thanksgiving holiday suddenly looming large and lonely ahead of her.

Beth walked to the table and sat in the chair across from her. "And when Evie grows up?"

"Then you and I can have this talk again." She fidgeted with a pen, spinning it in a pinwheel on the table.

Beth's eyes turned sad. "I'll respect your need for privacy." Standing again, she started to return to the front desk, then looked back over her shoulder. "Oh, in case you wanted to tell the Cattleman's Club thank-you in person, this weekend they're having a big cleanup in preparation for Christmas decorating."

Whit couldn't remember having a crummier Thanksgiving. Thank God it was finally over and he could spend the weekend helping out at the club with cleanup and decorating.

His invitation to spend Thanksgiving with Megan and her daughter had been impulsive— he'd originally just planned to send some flowers as part of his gradual pursuit. So he'd been surprised at the level of disappointment when she'd turned him down for dinner. That frustration had gathered steam with each day he waited and she didn't return his calls.

His catered turkey meal had tasted like cardboard. He'd ended up donating the lot to a homeless shelter. There had been invitations from his buddies in the Cattleman's Club to join them and their families for the holiday, but he hadn't felt up to pretending. No doubt part of his bad mood could be chalked up to the memorial service planned for Craig next week.

He just wasn't up to being everyone's pal today, either, but he'd promised to help and so many of them had chipped in to volunteer at the shelter. This club was the closest thing to family he had.

Launched by some of the most powerful men in town, the Texas Cattleman's Club had stood proud in Royal, Texas for more than a century. The TCC worked hard to help out in the community while also being a great place for members to get away from it all and to make contacts.

To be invited into the TCC was a privilege and a life-long commitment. And for a man who'd grown up as rootless as he had, that word—commitment—was something he didn't take lightly.

He climbed a ladder to hook lights along a towering tree outside the main building, an old-world men's club built around 1910. The tree was taller than the rambling single-story building constructed of dark stone and wood with a tall slate roof. Part of that roof had been damaged by the tornado, as were some of the outbuildings.

Looking in through the wide windows, he could see other club members and their families decorating the main area, which had dark wood floors, big, leather-upholstered furniture and super-high ceilings. TCC president Gil Addison was leading a contingent carrying in the massive live tree to be used inside.

What would Megan think of all the hunting trophies on the wall? He'd never thought to consider her feeling on that subject given her work in animal rescue. But he sure as hell hoped it wasn't a deal breaker.

He hooked his elbow on the top of the ladder, looking out over the stable, pool, tennis courts and a recently added playground. Evie would love this place. He could almost envision her in her tiara, fitting right in with the rest of the kids. Except a person had to be a member to have full use of the facilities.

How had he gotten to the point in his mind where he was envisioning Evie and Megan here?

"Whit?"

A voice from below tugged his attention back to the present.

He looked down to find one of his pals from the Dallas branch of the TCC, Aaron Nichols, partner in R&N Builders. Aaron had been overseeing the repairs to the club, but didn't appear to be in any more of a merrymaking mood than Whit was. But then given the fact Aaron had lost both his wife and his kid in a car accident several years ago, Whit could see how holidays must be particularly tough.

Which made him a first-class ass for feeling sorry for himself over being alone for Thanksgiving.

Whit hooked the lights along the top of the tree, wrapping and draping. "Hey, buddy, what can I do for you?"

Aaron handed up more lights, controlling the strand as it unrolled. "Just here to help. Shoot the breeze. Everyone's asking about you inside."

"Yeah, well, somebody's gotta take care of the tree out here." That had always been Craig Richardson's job.

Aaron nodded with an understanding that didn't have to be voiced. "Have fun on your big rescue mission?"

As if Whit hadn't been asked that question a million times already. Folks had expected him to bring Megan today. He'd entertained that notion himself while in Colorado, but she'd shut him down.

"We helped place a lot of cats, eased the burden on the shelter. It was a good day." He kept the answer brief and changed the subject. "Thanks for the cleanup at the shelter last weekend." Whit hooked the light over a branch. "I appreciate so many of you pitching in."

"We help our own," Aaron said with a military crispness he hadn't lost in spite of getting out of the service. "We would have gone sooner if we'd realized how tough things were at the shelter."

And Megan wasn't one to ask for help easily. He admired her independent spirit, her grit, the way she fought for her daughter and the animals. He just hadn't realized how much he would flat-out enjoy being with her too.

He hauled his attention back to the present rather than daydreaming like a lovesick teenager. "Everyone's been up to their necks in repairs. Sometimes it's difficult to tell where to start."

As he reached for Aaron to feed him more lights, Whit caught a glimpse of a car approaching with a woman at the wheel.

There was a time when women weren't allowed at the club unless they were accompanied by a male member. But a few years ago the TCC had started allowing women to join, a huge bone of contention that caused great friction in the organization.

Now, however, almost ten percent of its members were females. Two years ago they'd added an on-site day-care center, which had created even greater discord. But this year, things had finally begun to settle down and feel normal for the TCC members. Watching everyone pull together today, Whit could see there was a real sense of camaraderie the club hadn't experienced in a long time.

So a woman coming to the club on her own wasn't a surprise or big deal. Except this woman had unmistakably red hair. Whit knew her from gut instinct alone, if not sight. His pulse sped up and he decided that this time, he wouldn't just bide his time. He'd known and wanted her for years. Aaron Nichols's presence had served to remind him how fast second chances could be taken away.

Whit tossed aside the strand of lights, leaving them tangled in the tree branches for now, and climbed down the ladder. Because he'd found the perfect distraction to lift his holiday mood and make him feel less like Scrooge.

Megan Maguire had come to the Texas Cattleman's Club.

# Six

Megan told herself she was not coming to the Cattleman's Club to see Whit. Absolutely *not*.

Holding a Tupperware container full of home-made brownies, she exited her new-used compact purchased after the tornado took out her other car and hip-bumped the door closed.

Evie had wanted to bake on Thanksgiving so they would be like a real family. Real? The comment had sent Megan into a frenetic Betty Crocker tailspin that produced dozens of brownies.

She was proud of the life she'd built, damn it. She was an independent woman with a satisfying career and a great kid.

This morning hadn't been very easy though. Evie had thrown a screaming fit over the thought of wearing regular clothes to a playdate with Miss Abigail's great nieces. The counseling videos and books recommended by the preschool director just weren't working with Evie. Finally, Megan had surrendered to the request for a homemade costume made out of cut up sheets. In the big-picture view of things, it was most important that Evie wanted to play with other kids again without her mom present. But Megan had had to draw the line somewhere. When Evie had wanted to be a zombie, Megan suggested she be a mummy instead. Somehow a mummy princess seemed more benign than a zombie princess. What four-year-old knew about zombies?

Megan adjusted her hold on the container of brownies and picked her way around the big trucks and SUVs in the parking lot. Halfway to the looming lodge, as she was passing a golf cart loaded down with fresh evergreen boughs and spools of red ribbon, she felt as if she was being watched. She tracked the sensation to a towering pine tree with a ladder beside it. Whit stood at the base, his boot on the bottom rung, Stetson tipped back on his head.

Of course she'd known he would be here today.

But she didn't know what she would say to him. At all. She'd been off-kilter this week, questioning herself. She'd spent all of Thanksgiving imagining what it would have been like to share the day with him. Had he been alone on the holiday because of her decision?

His offer to spend the day together had intrigued her the more she thought about it. But it also had her reliving their kiss in Colorado. Had she really thought she could just sleep with him for one night and then walk away? This was a small town. They would run into each other.

Often.

That was good motivation to tread warily, because if things exploded between them, there could be lasting fallout. Not just the upheaval it would cause for Evie to lose a male figure in her life, but Megan also had to think of her job and how a big blow-up between her and Whit could make living in this town together awkward. She had to put Evie first and her daughter was happy here.

"Hey, hello, Megan," a female voice called out from a row of cars over.

Megan turned to see Stella Daniels waving as she got in her sedan to leave. The administrative assistant from the mayor's office had become an unexpected hero after town hall had taken a direct hit in the tornado. With Mayor Richard Vance still in the hospital, Stella was serving as the unofficial leader of Royal, giving interviews to the major networks and making heartfelt pleas for federal aid. Her quiet calm was just what the town needed in a crisis.

Megan could use some of that calm for herself.

Waving back, she smiled, then grappled to keep the plastic container from tumbling out of her arms. Stella ducked into her car; the organized woman was likely headed back to the office or off to inspect more cleanup efforts, even on the weekend.

Megan balanced the brownies again, turning back to the ladder only to find Whit gone. But it wasn't more than a second before Whit's broad hands came into view, sliding underneath the container.

"Can I help you with that?" he asked, his broad flannel-clad shoulders angling beside hers, their elbows bumping lightly as he shifted to help.

"Thank you. I brought these to thank the club for all their hard work at the shelter." She handed the three dozen turtle brownies to Whit.

"That's what we do." He glanced back over his shoulder. "Right, Aaron?"

Startled, she looked past Whit, surprised she hadn't even noticed Aaron Nichols was there as well. Just as she hadn't noticed Stella until the woman had called out. Megan had been one hundred percent focused on speaking to Whit. She'd seen that easy smile too many times in her dreams. Remembered the feel of his touch on her waist. Her hips…

Aaron clapped a hand on Whit's shoulder. "We can finish up later." He tipped his head to Megan. "Good to see you, Megan. Be sure this bozo doesn't keep all the brownies for himself. See you inside." He pivoted away and went into the lodge.

And then Megan was alone with Whit for the first time since before Thanksgiving. She searched for something to say to fill the awkward silence, finally asking, "What was Stella Daniels doing here?"

She tried not to let her gaze roam all over Whit. No easy task, that.

"She came to ask for help out at town hall. They're still plowing through debris and there's concern about lost files."

"If anyone can restore order in the chaos, Stella can." The town was lucky to have someone so competent leading recovery efforts during such a tumultuous time. "She's done some great work in organizing reconstruction during the mayor's recovery."

Mayor Vance had suffered massive injuries while working out of the town hall when the tornado hit. Stella seemed unsure of herself at times, but she was proactive in rounding up help where it was needed. And the Cattleman's Club was definitely the place to check, full of powerful movers and shakers in the community.

"The club is all in to do what we can." Whit's

molten brown eyes held her for another long instant, making her skin tingle. "How was your Thanksgiving?"

She swallowed hard, thinking about how she'd been too much of a coward to return his calls. "Evie and I had a feast of chicken nuggets and sweet potato fries, then made turkey paintings using our handprints. The front of my refrigerator is full of artwork." She paused for an instant before asking, "How was your Thanksgiving?"

"Lonely," he said simply, without even a hint of self-pity, more like a statement of fact.

Surprise kicked through her, quickly followed by guilt that he'd spent the day alone after reaching out to her. "You didn't spend the day with friends?"

"They have families, like you do." He shrugged his broad shoulders. "But hey, it wasn't a total wash. I watched ball games and ate a catered meal."

The Whit she'd spent time with recently, the Whit who was standing here with her now, didn't fit the image of the man she'd known for over three years. She wasn't sure what to make of him now. She'd been so sure he was a wealthy, ruthless charmer.

Maybe he really was just a nice guy who wanted to be with her. What the hell was wrong with her that she'd been upset because the man had acted like a gentleman and didn't jump all over her during their trip? "I'm sorry you spent the day alone. After all you did for the shelter it was small of me not to include you in my Thanksgiving."

"I didn't want you to include me in your holiday out of gratitude." He looked past her, trees rustling overhead. "Where's Evie today?"

"Playing with Miss Abigail's great nieces." She took the brownies back from him under the guise of securing the lid but really to occupy her jittery hands. It had been Evie's idea to give the extra brownies to Whit, but Megan had been wary of showing up on his doorstep. Bringing baked goods to the whole Club offered her a face-saving option.

A smile played with his mouth, a sexy mouth that kissed like sin. "What's our princess dressed as today?"

*Our?* Had he noticed the slip of the tongue?

"She wanted to be a zombie, but I thought that was a little dark for a kid that young. We opted for a mummy, like 'Monster Mash.'"

"Good call." He frowned, his hand tucking under the brim of his Stetson to scratch his head before he settled the hat back into place. "She's still having a tough time?"

"I've talked to the day-care director about it. Sue Ellen suggested some videos and books with tips on how to promote discussion with a child after a traumatic experience. I have the name of a counselor too." She swallowed hard. "I hope we won't need to use it. I figured I would give her another week to ease back into a routine. Hopefully she'll get excited about Christmas celebrations at school."

"Hopefully," he echoed.

She should go. She reached and opened the container, releasing the intoxicating scent of chocolate. "Would you like an advance sampling of the brownies as an olive branch? Well, a chocolate kind of olive branch?"

She took one out to offer it.

He leaned in to bite off a corner of the brownie

while she still held it. "Hmmm…" He hummed his appreciation as he chewed. "Damn, these are good."

His praise warmed her on a chilly day. "I'll take that as a compliment, coming from a man who can afford to eat at the best of the best restaurants."

"The cooking service I use has never brought anything as good as this." He popped the rest of the brownie in his mouth and reached for another.

"Over-the-top flattery." She scrunched her nose and set the container aside on the golf cart. "That can't be true."

"Sure it is." His smile was as bright as the dappled sunlight in the tree branches. "A cooking service is a luxury, but it's a necessity for me unless I want to eat at a restaurant every night, which I do not. I get to kick back in front of my television at night like a normal guy."

"A normal guy with a cooking service." She toyed with a strand of lights dangling off the cart.

"A cooking service I may have to fire since apparently they have been feeding me substandard brownies."

Damn it. How could she not like a guy who said things like that? She couldn't hide a smile.

"Evie and I will make some more just for you to thank you for the flight." The offer fell from her mouth before she could overthink it.

"I should say no, given how busy you are. But I'm going to be utterly selfish and accept." He finished off the second brownie.

"It's the least I can do after all your help. And you were so patient with Evie last weekend."

"That's a good thing. So why are you frowning?"

And there was the crux of things, her real reason for coming here with the brownies when she knew she would run into Whit. "My daughter is hungry for a father figure in her life. I just don't want her to build false hopes based on some nice gestures from you."

"Is that why you turned down my request to spend Thanksgiving together?" He raised an eyebrow.

"Yes, in part," she said carefully.

"You gotta know I think she's a great kid and I enjoy her company as well."

Yet another reason to like Whit. His affection for Evie was genuine.

Megan sagged back against a fat oak tree, bark rough even through her thick sweater and jeans. "She's a kid in a fragile state of mind. I'm not… comfortable risking anything upsetting her."

"Okay, okay…." Exhaling hard, he pressed a hand to the tree trunk, just above her head. "I can see where you're coming from on that, given the tiara and tornado-butt-kicking costumes."

"I'm glad you understand my predicament. I'm her mother. I have to put her needs first."

"You're a great mom too, from everything I've seen." His head angled closer. "I have to wonder though. Why did you kiss me in the hotel? Call me arrogant, but I wasn't mistaken in thinking you're interested…." He stroked her loose hair back over her shoulder. "Unless you were using me as a one-night stand. In which case you should be upfront about that. I'm not passing judgment. Just asking for honesty."

His touch sent a shiver down her spine. "Point taken."

"Exactly." His hand glided down to her shoulder blade, his fingers tangled in her hair.

Thank heaven everyone was inside, though the possibility that someone could catch sight of them through a window helped keep her in check. And heaven knew she needed all the help she could get to restrain her from throwing herself at him again. Her daughter's well-being had to be first and foremost in her mind.

"Whit, I'm just asking you not to use her to get to me. She's a little kid who still believes in fairy tales where princesses can always win in the end."

"What about her mom?" He cupped the back of her neck, massaging lightly. "What does *she* believe in?"

His question stunned her silent for three heartbeats. "What does that matter?"

"Because, honest to God, I want to get to know you better."

His words filled the space between them with so much hope and possibility, she was scared as hell to step out on that ledge and risk a big fall.

So she settled for sarcasm. "You want to sleep with me."

"True enough." He eased his hand around to palm her cheek, caressing with his thumb. "Can you deny you're attracted to me?"

"Your ego is not your most attractive quality."

He chuckled softly. "What is, then?"

"Searching for compliments?" She tipped her chin. "I wouldn't have expected that from you."

He ducked his head. "Megan, I'm searching for a way to get through to you, because make no mistake, I want to spend more time with you. A lot more. I always have." His words and eyes were filled with sincerity. "I was able to keep my distance when I thought the feeling wasn't mutual. But now that I know you're attracted to me too? I'm all in."

Her breath hitched in her chest. "What does that mean?" Nerves made her edgy.

"A regular date, dinner with me."

Dinner scared her a lot more than the notion of no-strings sex. "I can't leave Evie alone and she can't stay out that late."

"What time does she go to sleep?"

She chewed her bottom lip, already seeing where he was going with this. "At eight."

"Then how about getting a sitter and we go out after she falls asleep."

"And this gossipy small town we live in?"

"There are plenty of places other than Royal to find dinner. We can get to know each other better talking during the drive."

She hesitated, wanting to agree but unable to push the words past her lips.

A smile stretched across his handsome face, giving him a movie-poster twinkle in his eyes. "I'll take that as a yes. See you tomorrow at eight-fifteen." Stepping back, he picked up the brownies again. "Let's take these inside so we can get started making plans for the evening."

The next day, after finishing up at the Cattleman's Club, Whit rushed home to shower and make plans for his evening with Megan. God, he needed her and not just for the distraction of forgetting about Craig's upcoming memorial service. But for the chance to be with her, talk to her, find out why she had this tenacious hold over his thoughts.

She'd clearly had reservations, but she'd still agreed. She'd been emphatic though that he couldn't arrive until after eight once she had Evie in bed.

As if he didn't understand how important it was to be careful of the little girl's feelings.

But one victory at a time.

He finished his shower and pulled out a suit, more ramped for this date than he could remember being...ever.

An hour later, he shifted his sports car into park outside Megan's cute three-bedroom bungalow south of downtown. He'd left the truck at home tonight and opted for his silver Porsche. He wanted to make the evening special for her. He had things back on track to win Megan over. Tonight was a big step in the right direction.

He'd considered bringing her flowers, but didn't want to be obvious. So he'd opted to buy her a catnip plant. He'd actually bought two, one for her and one for his greenhouse even though he didn't have a cat. He'd also picked up a citronella plant that repelled mosquitoes to give him an excuse to stop by the shelter.

Walking up the flagstone path, he took in the multicolored lights on the bushes and a little wooden sign that read *Santa, please stop here.* He climbed the steps and knocked twice just under the holly wreath on the door.

Dogs barked inside and he could hear Megan shushing them just before she opened the door. The sight of her damn near took his breath away. She wore a Christmas-red dress, the wraparound kind with a tie resting on her hip. Those strings made his fingers itch to untie the bow, to sweep aside the silky fabric and reveal the hot curves underneath. His gaze raked down her body, all the way to her bare feet, that tiny paw tattoo on her ankle tempting him all the more.

And he would have told her just how incredible she looked with her hair flowing loose to her shoulders except two dogs ran circles around his legs. He planted one hand on the door frame and gripped the terra-cotta pot with the catnip plant in the other. Some kind of Scottie mix in an elf sweater yapped at him while a border collie bolted out around the porch, then back inside.

"Sorry for the mayhem." Megan rolled her eyes. "Piper and Cosmo just need a good run in the back yard before I go."

"No problem." He passed her the plant. "Catnip."

"Thank you, how thoughtful. Truffles, Pixie and Scooter will have a blast with it." Her smile was wide and genuine, her lips slicked with gloss. "Come on inside. Evie is asleep and Abigail should be here soon to watch her. Beth helps out, but since she's with your friend Drew…I just want to keep any talk to a minimum."

He swept off his Stetson as she stepped aside to let him in. He focused on learning more about her from her house to distract himself from the obvious urge to keep staring at her.

Her home was exactly how he would have imagined: warm and full of colors. A bright red sectional sofa held scattered throw pillows and three cats. Her end tables were actually wood-encased dog crates. A toy box overflowed in a corner.

And there were photos everywhere. Of her with Evie. Of them with the dogs. The cats too. Years of her life not just on the mantel but also in collages on the walls.

She held up the sprig of catnip. "I'm just going to water this."

He followed her into the kitchen and sure enough, the refrigerator front was decorated in finger-painted turkeys and a cotton ball snowman. He noticed her recycling station tucked just inside the laundry room, with its neat stacks of bundled newspapers and rinsed milk jugs in labeled bins. "I should take lessons from you on recycling."

"You should," she said pertly.

Chuckling softly, he looked past all those precise labels, and saw a large crate with a familiar calico cat inside.

"Is that the same cat I brought to the shelter?" He pointed. "Tallulah? I thought she was staying in your office."

"Tallulah came down with an upper respiratory infection, so I brought her home to keep a closer watch over her." She turned off the water and set the plant on the counter. "I've been crating her to keep her separate from the other animals."

He knelt beside the extra-large enclosure, wriggling his fingers through the wire. The kitty woke, arching her back into a long stretch. She was a damn cute little scrap. "Is she going to make it?"

"She's doing much better now." Megan leaned a hip against the doorframe, crossing her arms over her chest as she watched him with curious eyes. "She's on medication. I've been keeping her at home with me at night to make sure she's eating and hydrated."

As if on cue, Tallulah went to the double bowl and lapped up water.

Whit stood again, inhaling Megan's cinnamon scent. "Do you often take animals home from work?"

"We all do. There are never enough foster homes, especially right now."

"And I added to that burden by bringing in Tallulah. I'm sorry about that."

"You're a confusing man, Whit Daltry." She studied him intently.

"If it makes you feel better, I'm not even close to understanding you yet either. But everything I've seen so far, I like." Unable to resist for another second, he tipped his head and brushed his mouth against hers.

The soft give of her lips and that sweet moan of hers had him reaching for her. She didn't lean in, but she wasn't pulling away either. So he moved slowly, carefully. And savored the feel of her.

He slid his hands behind her, along her waist, the silkiness of her dress teasing his hand with thoughts of how silky her bare skin felt. He tasted her, drawing her closer and just enjoying the moment. Things couldn't go any further, not with the babysitter due to knock on the door at any second.

So he enjoyed just kissing Megan, learning more about the way the two of them fit together. Her arms slid around his neck and she pressed those sweet curves against him as her fingers toyed with his hairline. Such a small gesture, but each brush of her fingertips sent his pulse throbbing harder through his veins.

He backed her against the door and she stroked

her foot up the back of his calf. A growl rumbled in the back of his throat, echoing the roar in his body to have this woman, to take her even though his every instinct shouted he would lose her if he moved too fast.

The doorbell rang, jarring him back to his senses.

For now.


A date.

She was on a no-kidding, grown-up date.

Megan couldn't even bring herself to feel guilty. Her child was asleep and well cared for and she was enjoying an adult evening out with a sexy, fascinating man.

The valet drove away to park the Porsche as she and Whit climbed the steps of the restored mansion-turned-restaurant. She had heard about the French cuisine at Pierre's, but never had the spare cash or free time to try it for herself. Her heels clicked on her way up the stairs and she couldn't miss the way Whit's eyes lingered on her legs.

A rush of pleasure tingled through her.

Sure, she loved being a mom and enjoyed her

job, but it was nice to slip into a dress that wasn't covered with ketchup or cat hair. She tucked her hand into the crook of Whit's arm as they stepped over the threshold into the warm, candlelit restaurant. Her fingers moved against the fine weave of his suit jacket.

A string quartet played classical carols in the foyer, elegant strains swelling up into the cathedral ceiling. She was so preoccupied with taking it all in she almost ran smack dab into an older couple. She started to apologize, then realized— damn it—they weren't the only Royal residents who'd ventured outside the city limits.

She forced herself to relax and smile at Tyrone and Vera Taylor. "Good evening. Imagine running into you two here."

She'd hoped to keep her relationship with Whit out of the public eye a while longer, but she should have known that would be next to impossible, in most any local restaurant given their wide circle of friends.

"Whit?" Tyrone said. "What are you—? Oh, well, hello, Ms. Maguire."

"Good evening, sir," Whit answered the silver-haired man. Tyrone had a reputation for riding roughshod over people, but Whit met him face on without a wince.

Megan considered asking them about their newborn grandbaby in the NICU, about their daughter Skye still in a coma, but rumor had it Vera wasn't enthused about being a grandmother. The possibility of that poor little baby being unwanted hurt Megan's already vulnerable heart. So she simply said, "You and your family are in my thoughts."

"Thank you," Vera answered tightly before turning to her husband. "Tyrone?"

The blustery man clapped Whit on the shoulder. "We'll let you get to your meal. I'll see you at the town hall cleanup…and of course at Craig Richardson's memorial service."

"Yes, sir." Whit nodded curtly.

Megan wondered if the others noticed the tension in Whit's shoulders at the mention of his dead friend. She tucked her hand into the crook of his arm again and squeezed a light reassurance.

The maître d' arrived and saved them from further awkward conversation by leading the Taylors to their table while the hostess guided Whit and Megan to theirs—thankfully on the other side of the room.

Megan settled into her seat, the silver, crystal and candlelight a long way from chicken nuggets and fast food on the run. Music from the quartet filled the silence between them until their waiter took their order. They both settled on the special: rack of lamb, white grits and Texas kale.

As she stabbed at her salad, she realized just how quiet Whit had gone and knew with certainty that the mention of his friend Craig had hit him hard.

"Are you okay?" She rested a hand over Whit's. "We don't have to do this tonight."

"I want to be here with you." He flipped his hand over to squeeze hers. "I'm good."

"You don't have to be Mr. Charming all the time." In fact, she sometimes wanted a sign to know what was real about him, what she could trust, because lately he seemed too good to be true. "We can call it a night and reschedule."

His thumb caressed along the sensitive inside

of her wrist. "No. I need a distraction and you're a damn fine one."

"Thank you, I think." She tipped her head to the side. "I'm just so sorry for your loss."

"Me too. It was just so...." The tendons in his neck stood out, and even in the dim candlelight, she could see his pulse throbbing along his temple. "Losing him in that tornado was just so unexpected."

She agreed on many levels. The whole town of Royal, Texas, had been tipped upside down by that storm. "Do you think we're both just reacting to all that life-and-death adrenaline?"

His gaze snapped up to meet hers. "What I feel for you has nothing to do with a natural disaster."

"But I kissed you that day and that changed things between us."

"Lady," a smile finally tugged at his handsome face, "I was attracted to you long before that kiss."

She'd suspected, but hearing that gave her a rush far headier than it should have. "I thought I was just a great big pain in the butt since I moved to town."

He glanced down again. "Craig used to tell me I should just sweep you off your feet."

"You told him how you felt?"

Whit shook his head. "I didn't have to. Craig guessed. He said it was obvious every time I looked at you." And his eyes held hers again now, full of heat and intensity. "But you shut me down cold right from the start. And I can't blame you. We had our disagreements. I thwarted your business plans. And you were quite vocal in your disapproval of my company buying wetlands. I thought I was saving us both a lot of grief by steering clear. Then you kissed me, and all bets were off. I would have acted sooner but when we got the news about Craig…."

The confirmation that he'd been wanting a relationship with her for so long rattled her more than a little. "You've been grieving."

"I have…still am." He glanced down for a couple of heartbeats before swallowing hard and looking back up at her. "But that doesn't stop life from happening. And it doesn't stop me from thinking about what happened between us that day. We can't ignore it."

Her face flamed. "I'm embarrassed that I kissed you."

"But you liked it." He leaned back in his chair, watching her over the candlelight. "So did I."

She couldn't deny it to him or to herself any longer. She wanted Whit, and she wanted him for more than just one night. "Obviously I liked it."

He leaned closer, took her hand across the table, the heat in his eyes smokier than the candle between them. "Then let's do it again."

# Seven

After Whit's suggestive comment, dinner had passed in a blur of anticipation as she waited for this moment. To be in Whit's sports car heading to his house. To be alone. Together.

A part of her knew she'd done a grave disservice to the fine cuisine, but she could only think of the promise in Whit's eyes. Now they were finally at his house for after-dinner drinks and whatever else came next.

The garage door slid closed behind them, sealing them inside one of the four bays, where they were surrounded by other signs of his luxurious lifestyle. She'd seen the truck, but there was also a boat. A motorcycle. She gulped back a nervous shiver and concentrated on the man in the seat next to her instead. He was about more than expensive toys and an extravagant lifestyle. Whit was real. This was real. She was going to act on her feelings for this man. The attraction that had been simmering between them for days—weeks, years—would finally be fulfilled. She'd ached for him, dreamed of him.

Shifting in her seat, she smoothed her fingers over the red silk hem where it had ridden up one knee just a little. She'd dressed with care, wanting to be noticed. Yet the silk fabric had teased her too, clinging and skimming along her skin every time she moved.

Whit turned to her, the leather seat creaking. Her temperature spiked and heart pounded. She met his gaze and knew what was coming. She'd been waiting all evening....

He sketched his mouth over hers lightly. Once. Twice. Nipping her bottom lip and launching a fresh shower of sparks through her veins.

Then he eased back and looked into her eyes.

"Going inside doesn't commit to anything more than you want."

She angled her head to the side and lifted an eyebrow. "Really? Are you going to kiss and bolt again?"

"Not a chance." He tucked his hand behind her head, his fingers massaging a sensual promise into her scalp. "I just want you to know I care about you."

The simple words were filled with layers of meaning she wasn't ready to delve into just now. Still, she held them close, savoring the heady warmth of being cared about by this handsome, magnetic man.

"I want to see the inside of your house." She stroked his face with one hand and reached for her door handle with the other. "So let's go."

"Yes, ma'am." He scooped up his Stetson. "I'm happy to oblige."

As she stepped out of the low-slung sports car, Whit was already holding the door open for her like the perfect gentleman he'd been all evening. His palm low on her back, he guided her past his Porsche and truck toward the door. The warmth of his hand seared through her silky dress. The silence wrapped around her as they climbed the three stairs into his house.

And holy cow, what a house.

*Mansion* would be a more appropriate word. She slipped off her heels and padded barefoot down the corridor leading to the main foyer. She wriggled her toes against cool marble, then into the plush give of a Persian rug. She tipped her head back to stare up the length of the stairway, up to the cathedral ceiling with a crystal chandelier. The scent of lemony furniture polish and fine leather teased her nose. Whit stood silently at her side.

God, the place was quiet compared to the constant mayhem of her home, with Evie's laughter, dogs barking, and kids' television shows playing. Curious to learn more about this man full of contradictions, Megan glanced at the dining room to her left, with its heavy mahogany table set, then turned to the living room on her right. She stepped through the archway, taking in the tan leather sofas and wingbacks, tasteful while still being oversized for a man. She trailed her fingers along the carved mantel above the fireplace.

"What do you think?" he asked from behind her, his footsteps thudding on the hardwood floor.

"It's…" She searched for a word to describe the surroundings that had clearly been professionally decorated, just as his meals were professionally prepared. The place was pristine. High-end gorgeous. Yet missing all the touches that made a place a home. There was no clutter, no scars on the furniture from the wear and tear of making memories.

And there were no pictures, just knickknacks on the shelves and gallery artwork on the walls. But no photos. That tugged at her heart as sad, so very sad. "You have a lovely home."

His hands fell to rest on her shoulders, his chin against her hair. "It's a damn study in beige and I never realized that until I compared it to your place tonight. Kinda like how your brownies taste better than anything the best catering service could offer."

With every word, he made her heart ache more for him. She turned in his embrace and slid her arms around his neck. She saw so much in his eyes. So much caring and even a hope for things she wasn't sure she could give him.

But she couldn't think about that now. She refused to ruin this night by borrowing trouble from what might come. For now, she just wanted to enjoy this new connection and all the heady promise of his touch.

She stroked the back of his neck along his close-cropped hairline. "Do you really want to talk about paint swatches and recipes? Because I have something a lot more interesting in mind." She gripped his shoulders, her fingers flexing against hard male muscle. "The only question in my mind is, do you prefer the leather sofa or your bedroom?"

Megan's proposition fueled Whit's already smoldering need for her. Dinner had been a delicious torture as he waited to get her in his home, in his bed.

Although right now, the sofa sounded fine to him.

He skimmed the back of his fingers along her face. "You're sure this is what you want?"

"Are you kidding?" She tugged his hair lightly. "I thought I'd made my wishes abundantly obvious."

"I just want you to be clear." He cupped her face, resting his forehead on hers. "This won't be a one-night thing."

She hesitated, but only for an instant before whispering, "I hear you."

"And you agree." He needed to hear her say it. He'd waited too long to have this woman in his arms to wreck it all now.

"How about this." She angled closer into his embrace, her cinnamon scent filling his every breath. "It isn't a one-night stand, but we're still going to take it one night at a time."

He'd wanted more, but she hadn't said no outright. He was a smart man. He'd made progress, and he wasn't going to wreck his chance with this amazing woman.

He wrapped his arms around her and pressed her soft body to his. "I can live with that for now."

"Good, very good." She swept her hands into

his suit coat and shrugged his shoulders until the jacket fell to the floor. "Because you've been filling my dreams for a very long time."

"I would bet not as long as you've been in mine."

"Really?" Her green eyes went wide, her voice breathy. "Tell me more."

"Yes, ma'am. I'd heard about the hot new director at the shelter, then I saw you and you were—are—so much more than hot." He took a step toward the wide leather sofa, then another step. "But you shut me down cold because of the property dispute."

"I noticed you all right." She tugged at his tie, loosening it and pulling it free from his collar. "But yes, you made my life more than a little difficult by putting up roadblocks for the original shelter plans. And you're right that I don't approve of your company's history of buying up wetlands. But, to be honest, there's more. I was still wrapped up in getting my feet on the ground with Evie and being a mom."

"It didn't have to do with trusting men because of Evie's father?" he couldn't resist asking.

"This conversation is getting too serious." She backed toward the sofa, their feet synching up with each step. "Can we return to the part where you tell me I'm beautiful and I tell you I admire your abs?"

"You like my abs, do you?"

Her fingers stroked down again until she cupped his butt. "I like a lot about you, Whit Daltry."

"Nice to know." He leaned down to kiss her just as she arched up to meet him.

The taste of their after-dinner coffee mingled with the flavor of pure Megan. A taste he was coming to know well and crave more with each sampling.

Every time he held her, it was only more intense. He leaned forward at the same time she fell back. They landed on the leather sofa in a tangle of arms and legs and need. The sweet give of her curves under him sent desire throbbing through him, making him ache to be inside her. The silk of her dress as she writhed against him only tormented him with the notion of how much better her skin would feel. He wanted her now on the sofa and again upstairs. But he also wanted to make this moment perfect for her. No rushing.

Although that was getting tougher to manage with her tugging his shirt from his pants and working his belt buckle open. He toyed with the hem of her dress, his knuckles brushing the inside of her knee and drawing a husky moan from her lips.

He'd been fantasizing all evening long about untying her wraparound dress, and he intended to fulfill that fantasy. Soon. For now, he lost himself in the pleasure of kissing her, stroking along her creamy thigh. Taking his time. Taking them both higher and higher still until the need was a painful razor's edge.

Drawing in a ragged breath to bolster himself, he lifted off her. The image of her kissed plump lips, her flame-red hair splayed across the buff-colored sofa, was pinup magnificence.

She looked up at him with a question in her sparkling green eyes. She extended a hand. "Whit? Where are you going?"

"To carry you to my bedroom." He scooped her into his arms and against his chest.

Her gasp of surprise made him smile.

She got past her surprise quickly, though, and toyed with the top button of his shirt. "Luckily for both of us, that's exactly where I want to be."

He headed back into the foyer and past the stairs with long-legged strides that couldn't eat up the distance to the master suite fast enough.

Finally, finally, he crossed the threshold into his room. He'd never thought of it as more than a place to sleep. Houses—homes—weren't things to get attached to.

Just short of the four-poster bed, he set her on her feet. As she slid down his body, she thumbed free two more buttons on his starched cotton shirt.

She angled back as if to sit on the edge of the bed and he stopped her with a hand to the waist.

"Wait," he said, "we'll get there soon enough."

He dropped to his knees, his hands grazing over her breasts on his way to hug her hips. Her husky sigh urged him on as he eyed the tie of her dress, the loops right there for the taking, releasing. He took one end of the sash between his teeth. He looked up at her, holding her gaze with his. Her hands fell to his shoulders, but not to push him away. In fact, she swayed a bit, her fingers digging into his back, as if she was bracing herself to keep her balance. She dampened her lips with her tongue.

He tugged, slowly, imprinting the moment on his mind. Her dress parted and with a shrug of her shoulders she sent it slithering off into a pool at her feet. His breath lodged in his chest, then he exhaled in a long, slow sigh of appreciation.

The sweet swell of her breasts in red lace, the curve of her hips in crimson satin panties had him throbbing harder with the urge to be inside her. Now. And thanks to her bikini undies, he found the answer to his question about whether she was hiding more tattooed paw prints. She had a tiny trail along her hip bone. He took the edge of her panties in his teeth and let it lightly snap back into place.

"Megan, you are…beautiful beyond words. More than I even imagined, and what I imagined was already mighty damn awesome." His hands trembled as he reached to stroke her arms. Sure, he'd touched before but the feel of naked flesh was so much more intimate now that her curves were bared.

A flush swept over her lightly freckled skin. "And you, Whit, are seriously overdressed for the occasion."

She tugged him back up to stand again and un-buttoned his shirt the rest of the way, one deliber-ate move at a time, kissing each inch of exposed skin. Her licks and nibbles had him bracing a hand against one of the bed posts to keep from stumbling to his knees again. He kicked off his shoes while she made fast work of unzipping his pants and shoving them down and off. Her eyes widened with appreciation and she stroked the length of him. He gave up and let gravity take them both onto the mattress.

Whit laid her back on the bed, his bed. In his room. His house. Finally, he had her here after three and a half long years.

He stretched out on top her, hot flesh meeting flesh. Her curves melded to him, enticed him, made him ache all the more to be inside her.

The thick comforter gave underneath them. He stroked up the creamy satin of her skin, cupping her lace-clad breasts. Her nipples tightened against his palms. A low growl rumbled in his chest and he took one of those hard pebbles in his mouth, teasing and circling with his tongue through the fabric.

He reached a hand behind her and unhooked her bra. Then, yes, he took her in his mouth again, bare flesh this time, and she tightened with pleasure at the stroke of his tongue. Her fingers dug deeper into his shoulders, cutting tiny half moons in his skin.

The moment was so damn surreal. He'd been hoping for this chance to be with Megan since the day he'd met her. He'd held himself in check because she'd shut him down cold for so long.

She wasn't cold now. Not even close.

Megan matched him stroke for stroke, taste for taste, exploring him as he learned the landscape of her naked body. Each panting breath came faster and faster, hers and his, and he knew restraint was slipping away. He angled off her to reach into the bedside drawer and pull out a condom.

She smiled a thanks before plucking the packet

from him. She tore the wrapper open, her eyes intent but her hands trembling. He understood the feeling well. She pressed a hand to his shoulder and nudged him onto his back.

With a smooth sweep of her leg, she straddled his legs. Her fiery red hair tumbled over her shoulder in a gorgeous tangled mess of curls. He reached to cradle her breasts in his palms, his thumbs circling. Her eyes fluttered closed for a second before she looked at him again and rolled the condom over him, one deliberate inch at a time, never taking her eyes off him.

He cupped her hips and drew her closer until his erection pressed against her damp cleft. She rocked against him and his fingers dug deeper into her flesh. Much more and this would be finishing too soon.

He lifted her from him and lowered her back to the bed, sliding on top of her again. She hitched a leg around his, gliding her foot along his calf and opening for him. He nudged against the warm, moist core of her, pressing and easing inside with a growl echoed by her sigh. He thrust deeper as she arched up with a with gasping "yesss."

Her hips writhed against his, her arms looped around his shoulders and holding him close. She gasped and whispered in his ear, nonsensical words that somehow he understood. He moved inside her, the velvety clamp of her body around him so damn perfect. Like her.

The need to pleasure her, to keep her, pulsed through him along with each ragged breath. He linked fingers with her, their clasped hands pressing into the comforter as they worked together for release. Damn straight he'd been right to wait for her, because being with Megan was more than special. This woman had him tied in knots from wanting her.

And even as he chased the completion they both craved, he was already planning the next time with her, and the next. But first, he had to be sure she felt every bit as rocked by the moment as he did. Whatever it took. He pulled a hand free and hitched her leg higher around him, kissing and stroking as he filled her.

Her head dug back into the pillow, thrashing, her gasps coming faster and faster, the flush on her chest broadcasting how close she was to… flying apart in his arms.

She arched against him, her arms flinging up to lock tighter, draw him closer and deeper as she dug her heels in and rode through each shivering echo of her orgasm.

The bliss on her face sent him over the edge with her.

He growled as his release shuddered through him again and again, each ripple of pleasure reminding him how much and how long he'd wanted this woman.

And how damn important it was to keep her.

Good sex mellowed a person.

But great, incredible, unsurpassable sex?

That made Megan nervous. She'd been looking for a brief, no-strings affair. What she and Whit had just shared made an already complicated relationship even more tangled.

Megan sat on a barstool at Whit's kitchen island, wearing his white linen shirt, while the man himself foraged in the refrigerator. He'd tugged on a pair of jeans and nothing more and heaven help her, he offered up an enticing view. His perfect butt in denim…his broad, bare shoulders… She swallowed hard and looked away.

She'd just had the best sex of her life. She should be rejoicing. Instead, she kept thinking about all the ways this could go so horribly wrong. And if it did, that failure would be in her face every single day because living in such a small town made it all but impossible to ignore each other.

Regardless of her intention to keep things light, tonight was a game changer. She knew that. To protect herself and her daughter, Megan would have to tread warily. Easy enough to do since her feelings for him made her jittery.

For now? Her best move would be to get to know as much about him as possible and figure out quickly whether or not to run.

Whit grabbed two bottled waters and closed the refrigerator. He opened a cabinet and pulled out two cut crystal goblets. He poured them each a glass and set them on the island just as the microwave dinged. He'd warmed their crème brulee dessert they'd brought home rather than waiting any longer at the restaurant.

He snatched up a potholder, pulled out the warm pudding and placed it on the island. The image of him all domestic and sexy had her mouth watering.

She eyed the empty bottles and walked to the counter, letting her hip graze his as she passed. "I'll just toss these for you. Where's the recycling?"

"Thanks. Check the door beside the pantry."

She tugged open the door to reveal a line of high-end built-ins, labeled with brass plates. "Be still my heart. This is amazing."

She smiled over her shoulder at him, then opened the bin marked *glass*. She found it empty and pristine, clearly never used. She tamped down disappointment and tossed the two bottles inside. She turned back to find him standing right behind her with a sheepish grin on his face.

Whit slanted his mouth over hers. "Forgive me?" He kissed her again, then teased her bottom lip lightly between his teeth. "I promise to try to be more earth-friendly in the future. Scout's honor."

"I wish you would do it because it's a good

SHELTERED BY THE MILLIONAIRE

thing to do and not just to impress me." She enjoyed the bristle of his five o'clock shadow, savoring the masculine feel of him. "But I'll take the win for our planet however I can get it."

He chuckled softly against her mouth. "I appreciate your willingness to overlook my shortcomings."

His hands tucked under the hem of the shirt, cupping her hips in warm, callused hands. Goosebumps of awareness rose on her skin and she stepped closer, her feet between his as she flattened her palms to his bare chest. His heartbeat thudded beneath her touch, getting faster the longer the kiss drew out.

In a smooth move, he lifted her and set her on the island, his fingers stroking along her legs as he stepped back. "Food first. Then maybe we could share a shower—in the interest of conserving water, of course."

His promise of more hung in the air between them. He opened the silverware drawer and passed her a spoon.

Megan tapped the caramel crackle on top of the crème brulee, Whit's shirt cuffs flopping loosely around her wrists. "So I told you why I went into animal rescue. What made you decide to go into property development?"

He raised an eyebrow, his spoon pausing halfway to his mouth. "You say that like it's a something awful."

"I'm sorry. I didn't mean to sound…judgmental." She winced as she set her spoon down and folded back the shirt cuffs. "But I guess I wasn't successful in holding back."

"Well, I do have three and half years' worth of cold shoulders from you to go on."

"Help me to understand your side." She spooned up a bite and her taste buds sang at the creamy flavor. Of course, her senses were already alive and hyperaware after both of the spine-tingling orgasms Whit had given her.

"I like building things. I like helping businesses and people put down roots." He stood at the bar beside her, so close he pressed against her thigh.

"You can build things anywhere. Why destroy wetlands with high-rise office buildings?" Damn it. There came her judgmental tone again. But she had values. She couldn't hide what she believed in just because it might stir old controversies.

"I'm not destroying the wetlands around here." He said with an over-careful patience. "I'm relocating them, responsibly and legally. Tell me how that's a problem."

At least he was asking. He'd never opened the door to discussion before, just shut her down.

But then hadn't she done the same?

Now was her chance. "By relocating you're creating a manmade, imitation version of something that already exists in nature. Why not leave nature alone?"

He scooped up a spoonful of the crème brulee. "I guess we'll have to agree to disagree on the word imitation."

"You say you care about the animals and environment by relocating the wetlands." Frustration elbowed its way into her good mood. She set her spoon down and tried another approach to help him see her side of things. "In order to save animals, I needed the best facility and location possible, which you blocked. Legal and ethical aren't always the same."

He quirked an eyebrow. "You landed on your feet. The animals are cared for. I made sure of that."

"What?"

"I made sure the piece of land you ultimately built on was affordable."

She wasn't quite sure what to do with that piece of information. She rubbed a finger along the rim of her crystal goblet. "Are you saying you offered up a diversion so I would back away from the property you wanted?"

"Do we have to rehash this now?" He tempted her with another spoonful of his caramel custard dessert.

"I think we do." She took the spoon from him, licked it clean and set it down. "I would have been closer to Evie the day of the tornado if the shelter had been built where the original plan called for."

"Fine." He leaned back and crossed his arms over his chest. "I can't make business decisions based on personal convenience and be successful."

"I understand that. Obviously." She searched

his eyes for a sign of easing, but his expression was inscrutable. "But you also shouldn't pull your heart and humanity out of your job."

His eyes narrowed and chin tipped up as he reached to skim her hair over her shoulder, his hand lingering to stroke the sensitive spot behind her ear. "How can I make you get over that grudge?"

"I'm not sure. Show me you've changed…." She struggled to think, tough as hell to do with his touch enticing her to just sink into his arms again. "Or convince me you didn't do anything wrong."

"Megan," he said, exasperation dripping from that one word. Then he kissed her in an obvious attempt to distract her. "You're trying to pick a fight with me so I won't get closer. Am I wrong?"

His breath was warm along her face.

She whispered, "You're not wrong."

He nodded, then pulled back, his hand trailing along her arm. "Tell me how teaching your dog to ride a skateboard led you to become a shelter director rather than, say, a lion tamer?"

She grasped the safe topic with both hands,

grateful for the reprieve. "I was always the little girl bringing home stray kittens and lost dogs. My mother was terrified I would get bitten or scratched, and looking back I can totally see her point." She shrugged. "But nothing she said stopped me—you may have noticed, but I'm very stubborn. So my mom signed me up for this thing called 'Critter Camp' at our local Humane Society. It was a summer camp for kids. We learned about animal care, animal rights, responsible ownership and yes, animal rescue."

"Sounds like a great program."

"My mom had to work overtime to pay for it." The memory pulled her under, back to those days of her mother scrimping to support her child. Megan understood the fear and weight of that responsibility well. "I didn't realize that until I was older, begging to go to the camp for the fifth year in a row. But I was hooked. I looked into the animals' eyes and they needed me. But they also saw how much I needed them. People don't always realize that they save us just as much as we save them."

"Why haven't you started a critter camp here? I'm certain it would be a huge success."

A dark smile tugged at her mouth and she dropped a hand to his knee, squeezing. "Are you sure you want the answer to that?"

"I wouldn't have asked unless I wanted to know." His hand fell to her leg, his calluses rasping along her sensitive inner thigh.

She swallowed hard and tried to think past the delicious sensation. "Lack of space because of the plot of land we had to take as the consolation prize when you blocked the purchase of our original choice."

"You said you were content with the second location." Concern creased his forehead, but his hand inched higher.

She clamped his wrist. "It's farther from the schools, which makes logistics tougher for after-school programs. There are a host of other reasons—"

"Such as?"

"We need space to enlarge the dog park, and then there's the budget." She moved his hand back to the counter. "But if you start writing checks to the shelter and offering flights for animals, while generous, that does not buy you time with me. If you want to make a donation, I'll gratefully accept as the director. But we have to keep that separate from me—Megan, the woman."

He clasped her hand and brought it to his mouth, kissing her knuckles. "That said, will Megan, the *sexy* woman, have dinner with me again?"

Another brush of his mouth along the inside of her palm made it tough for her to think, but then that was a problem even when they weren't touching. She needed time to get her head together. She needed to figure out if it was even possible to let this play out regardless of the consequences.

That wasn't something she could figure out now. "I'm helping with the town hall cleanup tomorrow afternoon while Evie naps. We can talk about it then." She slid off the barstool. "I should get dressed and go home. I have to think about all that's happened between us."

He held on to her hand. "Remember what I said about one-night stands. I don't do them."

Could she trust in those words when neither of them knew what the future held? She searched his eyes and saw he believed what he said. For now.

Somehow that only made matters more complicated. "I remember." She let go. "I'll see you tomorrow—at town hall."

# Eight

The next day, Whit spent hours sifting through the rubble inside a town hall office, his buddy Aaron helping, but there was still no sign of Megan. This whole place was a lot like the mess of his life. His evening with Megan had been right on track. He'd been so certain they were making progress.

Then somehow things had derailed near the end for reasons that went a helluva lot deeper than his unused recycling bins. He still wasn't sure how they'd steered off course. It was as if they'd both self-destructed by discussing things guaranteed to drive a wedge between them.

And she still hadn't shown up for the town hall cleanup effort as they'd planned.

After their argument last night, they'd both thrown on their clothes and he'd driven her home, silence weighing between them in the dark evening streets. It was around one o'clock when they arrived, and he'd insisted on walking her to her door, where he gave her one more searing kiss. But she'd drawn the line there. She didn't want him to come inside where Abigail waited, babysitting Evie.

Work boots scuffling through dusty and crumbled brick, he took another garbage bag from Aaron. The job was too mindless to take his thoughts off Megan and what had happened last night. He trusted Abigail to keep her word to stay silent about their date until they—until Megan—was comfortable revealing the news to the town. But this had gone beyond Abigail. Given that they'd run into the Taylors at the restaurant last night, the whole town would know soon enough anyway.

As if there wasn't enough to keep everyone occupied. Like rebuilding the town.

The perimeter of town hall had been secured but there was no quick fix to all the destruction, especially inside in the few areas of the building still standing. Town hall had been almost totally destroyed. Only the clock tower had survived unscathed, but since the tornado, the time had been perpetually stopped at 4:14. The planning committee had decided to rebuild on the same location, but the cleanup effort would take time. They had to be careful sorting through the mess. Even in the digital age, there was so much damn paperwork.

Outside, Tyrone Taylor was barking orders to people as if it was his place to take charge. The guy seemed to think he ran the town. Luckily for them, Stella Daniels was there, and she had a quieter approach. A far more effective one at that. She let Tyrone bluster away and quietly followed up behind him giving direction and thanks.

Whit scanned the crowd outside the cracked window, over the parking lot, looking for Megan but she still hadn't shown. He hadn't heard from her since he'd driven her home. He'd called in the morning to offer her a ride over, but she hadn't answered. Was this a replay of the day the tornado hit when she'd shut him out after the kiss?

Being with Megan had been even more incredible than he'd expected. And his expectations had been mighty damn high.

He ground his teeth and focused on what he could fix. "Hey, Aaron, wanna help me lift this bookshelf and put it back against the wall?"

"Sure thing." Aaron squatted and braced both hands under one side of the walnut shelf. "Okay, Whit, on three, we lift. One. Two. Three."

Whit braced his feet, hefting and pushing alongside his friend until the bookcase was standing upright again. Files and thick hardbacks littered the floor where it had fallen. They were dry, but some had been soaked in the past, their pages curled and dirty brown. "We can put the undamaged items on the shelf again and stack the ruined stuff on the desk. The staff can decide what's crucial to keep."

"Sounds like a plan to me." Aaron scooped up two large volumes and paused, half standing, then pointed to the window. "Check out who just arrived—your shelter director lady friend."

Whit pivoted fast, then realized he'd given himself away with how damn eager he was just to see her. But he kept looking as she picked her way around a trash dumpster and a pile of broken boards. The sun streamed down on her fiery red hair, which was held back in a loose ponytail. Her jeans and shelter sweatshirt might as well have been lingerie now that he knew what was underneath. She could have been wearing a burlap sack and he would still want her.

Aaron stepped up beside him at the window. "So you and Megan Maguire have made peace with each other."

"We weren't at war." His denial came more out of habit than anything else; he was still focused on Megan, who was now talking to Lark Taylor, a local nurse passing out surgical masks for people to wear in the dusty cleanup.

"Like hell you two weren't constantly at odds," Aaron said. "You can't rewrite history, my friend. We all know how contentious things got over that land dispute when she wanted that site for the shelter. What I can't understand is how you got her to overlook how you buy up wetlands to build. She went ballistic last time it was mentioned."

As if Megan could hear their conversation—or feel the weight of Whit's stare—she turned, her eyes meeting his through the window with a snap of awareness as tangible as a crackle of static. He waved in acknowledgment, then turned back to cleanup detail. "We stay away from controversial topics these days."

Aaron didn't let him off the hook so easily. "Ah, you are seeing her. I always thought you had a thing for her under all that bickering."

Whit didn't like being transparent but he couldn't outright deny the obvious. "Why are you so all fired up to know about my personal life?"

"Oh, I get it. Who's trying to keep it quiet?" His friend elbowed his ribs like they were in freakin' high school. "You or her?"

Whit leveled a stare at his pal, who was grinning unrepentantly. "Do you want my help with this mess or not?"

"Somebody's touchy."

Touchy? That was one way to put it.

He was frustrated as hell that Megan appeared

to have returned to their old ways of avoiding each other. Damn it, last night had been a game changer.

Ignoring each other simply was *not* an option anymore.

Megan said bye to Lark and went in search of Beth. She wasn't sure if she wanted advice or a buffer, but she just wasn't ready to face Whit yet, and she couldn't stand out here shuffling her feet indefinitely.

A voice whispered in the back of her mind, asking her why she'd bothered to come here if she really wanted to avoid him.

Truth be told, Megan wanted to rush into town hall and find Whit, to touch him or even just look at him. And the strength of that desire was the very reason she had to stay away until she found her footing again. No man should have the power to rock her with just a simple glance through a window.

She needed to get her head on straight fast because given the way people kept looking at her and whispering to each other, she suspected that

Vera Taylor hadn't wasted any time in spreading the word about seeing her with Whit at the restaurant last night. Vera liked to pretend she was the expert on couples and marriage and everything else, but the senior Taylors were poster children for all the reasons marriage made people miserable.

But then on counterpoint, she saw the Holt family patriarch and matriarch bringing refreshments to the volunteers. Watching David and Gloria Holt lodged an ache in Megan's chest. Seeing them resurrected dreams she'd buried five years ago when Evie's father had walked out, leaving Megan pregnant and alone. The Holts were such a team, married for decades and still so deeply in love. Word around town was that David still brought his wife flowers every week. And Megan was glad Gloria had delivered her baked goods to boost the TCC's spirits after Megan's brownies. It was no contest: Gloria was renowned for her blue ribbon fruit pies.

Finally, she spotted Beth's blond head. Just last week, she and her friend had decided to create compost heaps for rubbish wherever possible. It wouldn't take care of all the recyclable debris, but it would help.

"Sorry I'm late," Megan said, kneeling beside a box of moldy computer paper that had been soaked by rain.

Beth swiped a wrist over her forehead, brushing back her hair. "The Holts are adorable, aren't they? Real soul mates."

"If you believe in that kind of thing, I guess." She tugged on the facemask Lark had given her and passed another to Beth.

Her friend pulled the elastic bands around her ears. "You don't believe in soul mates?"

"Years ago I did. I imagined finding him, getting married and starting a family." She looked up and shrugged, tossing a moldy ream of paper into the pile. "It's obvious things didn't work out that way. But I have my daughter. I love her and I don't regret having her for even a second."

But she couldn't deny life was tougher. Choices were more difficult.

"You don't mention Evie's father often. I've never wanted to pry, but it's tough not to feel judgmental of the guy when you're working so hard to do everything on your own."

"Thank God I found out what a selfish jackass he is before I married him." Still, the fallout for her daughter wasn't so clear-cut. "My only regret is the pain Evie will feel when she realizes he abandoned her. She doesn't ask about him now, but someday, she's going to want answers. Telling her he lives very far away won't be enough."

"There must have been some positives that drew you to him in the first place."

The oak tree branches rustled in the afternoon breeze as Megan tugged on work gloves. "I was blinded by his charm." She dug deeper into the rubble to move past bad thoughts. "He went out of his way to romance me with dinners and trips, gifts that seemed thoughtful as well as extravagant. It was like a Cinderella fantasy after the way I grew up."

"You're a big-hearted person who sees the best in people." Beth reached to give her arm a quick squeeze. "The only person I've ever heard you criticize is Whit."

"And people who abandon their animals." She scrunched her nose under the mask.

"Surely he ranks a level above them."

"Of course he does." Megan kicked through layers of dirt until she found more paper goods for the compost heap and some limp file folders that could go to the recycling pile. "I just don't want to repeat the past. I let myself believe in love at first sight. I was wrong. It takes time to get to know a person, to trust them."

"You've known Whit a long time." Beth loaded branches into a wheelbarrow for a bonfire later. "There's no issue with love at first sight here."

"I didn't say I love Whit Daltry." The L word. Her chest went tight. She tore off the mask to breathe deeper.

"I never said you did. You're the one who got defensive." Beth pulled off her surgical mask and guided Megan toward a park bench. "Where there's smoke, there's fire. And I'm seeing lots of smoke steaming off the two of you."

Megan sat down beside her friend, toying with the mask and snapping the elastic ear bands. "I've learned the hard way that attraction isn't enough. And I have Evie to consider now."

"You're not the only single mom to have been in this situation before, you know." Beth squeezed Megan's wrist. "There's happiness out there for you."

She looked out over the volunteers who'd turned up in droves, a town full of people who'd welcomed her into their fold. "I am happy with the life I've built."

"Fair enough. Still, there can be love and a partner for you. There can be a man who wants to be a father to that amazing daughter of yours. But you'll never know if you don't try."

Megan heard the logic in Beth's words, but accepting what she was saying was easier said than done. "I think we're all just feeling our mortality because of Craig and the others who died. We're all reacting out of grief and adrenaline, a need to affirm life."

"Or the tornado could have torn away your defenses and is making you face what you've been feeling all along."

"Okay, Dr. Freud." Megan bumped shoulders

with her friend. "Do you think we can back off analyzing for a while?"

The crunch of footsteps on downed branches gave her only a second's warning. She looked over her shoulder and found Whit approaching. Denim and flannel never looked so good. She smoothed back the wisps of loose hair into her ponytail before she could stop herself.

Beth stood abruptly as Whit leaned against the bench. "I think I'm going to head inside and see if Drew needs help. Good to see you, Whit." She scooped up her mask and jogged toward the clock tower.

The sounds of traffic being routed around town hall mixed with birds chirping. The world was almost normal again.

Almost.

Whit gestured to the scarred bench. "Mind if I sit?"

"Of course I don't mind." That would be silly, and she didn't even one hundred percent understand the turmoil inside her.

"I noticed that your car's blocked in so I'm offering you a ride if it's not clear when you're ready to leave." His hard thigh pressed against hers. He pointed to where utility vehicles had recently arrived and boxed in her compact.

She eyed him suspiciously. "Did you have something to do with my car getting blocked in?"

"Why would I do that?" He palmed his chest in overplayed innocence.

"You're funny." And she was being prickly for no reason. She rested her hand on his knee.

He covered her gloved hand with his. "Just trying to keep you happy. When are we going to make it official and tell folks we're seeing each other? They all know anyway."

Panic made it tough to breathe even without the surgical mask. "I need time to figure out what to tell Evie."

"Well, people are already talking so you should figure that out soon before someone says something in front of her."

"I know, I know." She sagged back on the bench, accepting she'd reached a crossroad with Whit. Beth's words knocked around in her mind. Had Megan just been hiding from her feelings for

Whit all along? She tugged off her work gloves. "We just need to be careful with Evie. She's fragile right now."

His thumb stroked the inside of her wrist. "Do you think she's going to be jealous of the time we spend together?"

"Just the opposite. She likes you." And that had a whole different set of potential landmines. "You're really good with her and that's scary too. Her heart's going to be broken when we—"

Irritation flickered through his dark brown eyes. "You're dooming this before we're even off the ground yet."

Was she? She reminded herself of the conversation with Beth. "I want to try. I just need time. Okay? Let's finish helping out and then you can drive me home if I'm still blocked in."

"Evie will be there. What will you tell her?"

She chose her words carefully. This was such a damn big step for her. She hoped he understood just how much. "That you're Mommy's very good friend." She tugged another surgical mask from her pocket and passed it to him. "Let's get back to work."

* * *

Whit hadn't had a role in blocking Megan's car but he was more than happy to ride the good luck that fate had dealt him. Now he had time alone with her to figure out why she was so spooked.

Not spooked enough to avoid him altogether though, because she could have asked Beth to bring her home. But she hadn't. Instead, Megan had worked beside him tirelessly at town hall, as if she didn't already carry a full load at the shelter, and agreed to a lift in his truck when they were done.

Sun dipping into the horizon, he pulled up and parked outside her cottage. "You fit right in here. You'd think you've lived here all your life."

"It's a welcoming town." She dusted off the knees of her jeans. She'd really dug in to help at town hall today.

She worked hard all the time and he couldn't help but want to make things easier for her.

Whit angled toward her, enjoying the way the setting sun brought out highlights in her hair. "Are you planning to stay in Royal?"

She blinked in surprise. "I don't have any plans to leave."

"That's not the same as planning to stay." He stroked a loose strand behind her ear.

"What about you?" she countered. "What if your business expands and there's a great opportunity to take things global or something?"

"No matter how large my company grows, Royal will always be where I've planted my roots," he said without hesitation. "This is the only place I've ever been able to call home. That's not something I'm willing to throw away."

She shook her head slowly. "Home is family, not a place. If I got an offer from another shelter for a significant pay raise, I would have to consider it, for Evie's future." She cupped his face. "Why are we discussing this now? It's a what-if that may not ever happen. Let's focus on this moment."

"Right, of course." His hand slid behind her head and he guided her to him and kissed her. It was just one of those simple kinds of kisses. But he was finding there were so many ways to savor this woman and they'd barely even begun.

She eased back and smiled. "I need to let Miss Abigail go. Do you want to come inside and have supper with Evie and me? It's nothing fancy. Just hot dogs, macaroni and cheese, maybe apple slices with peanut butter."

"Peanut butter?" He kissed her nose. "Now that's an offer I can't turn down." He stepped out of the truck.

She was trying, and that was more important than he wanted to admit to himself right now. He needed to keep his focus on the moment.

He followed Megan into her house, the warm space full of color and clutter reminding him again how his place didn't come close to feeling like a home. Tails wagging, Piper the Scottie and Cosmo the Border Collie raced across the room to sniff his shoes. The cats Truffles, Pixie and Scooter lounged on the back of the red sectional sofa in the same spots he'd seen them last time, as if they hadn't moved.

Evie jumped up from her Barbie house, wearing an angel costume with a halo and tiara, the two headpieces jumbled on top of each other. She ran to her mother and flung her spindly arms around Megan's waist. "Mommy, I missed you." She peeked up, a little bit of gold garland from the halo dropping over one eye. "Hello, Mr. Whit."

Miss Abigail scooped up her purse and sweater from the sofa beside one of the snoozing cats. "Well, hello, Whit. This is a surprise."

Megan kept her arms around her daughter. "My car was blocked in. Whit offered to bring me home."

"Right." Abigail winked. "Have fun, sweetie, and call if you need me to babysit. Anytime." She patted Whit on the cheek. "Treat her well."

The door closed behind the retired legal secretary. He took heart in the fact that Megan hadn't even bothered denying Abigail's assumptions.

Megan eyed him nervously, then blurted, "Would you mind keeping an eye on Evie while I change and cook supper?"

He could tell what that cost her. "Thanks, of course I can." He looked over at Evie's toys. "We'll play—"

"Tea party," the little girl squealed, and ran to the coffee table.

Megan's laugh tickled his ears as she left the room.

Whit sat on the sofa. "How's Tallulah?"

Evie arranged a tiny pink plate in front of him and one on her side, then placed two more on the table and whistled for Piper and Cosmo, both of whom were apparently familiar with the game and sat beside her. "My mommy's taking very good care of your kitty cat."

He didn't bother mentioning it wasn't his cat. From the mischievous glint in Evie's eyes, he suspected she was exerting some subtle pressure of her own. "Your mother is a very good person."

The little girl nodded her head and placed a plastic slice of cake on each plate. "My mom helps doggies and kitties."

"That's her job as a grown-up."

"I wanna job." She placed a saucer under each teacup then poured from the toy pitcher that made a *glub, glub, glub* sound.

"Your job is to learn your letters, to eat your vegetables and play."

"We are playing. Is the tea good?"

"Oh …." He pretended to sip from the cup that was smaller than a shot glass. "Very good."

She fished around in her pocket and pulled out two dollar bills and a quarter. "Mommy gave me this to buy treats when I go back to school. But I'm buying shoes for the kids that lost their shoes in the tora-na-do."

Whit set the tiny cup down carefully, his heart squeezing inside his chest at the weight this little girl was carrying on those small shoulders. Megan's words about having to be cautious for her daughter's sake rumbled around inside him.

"Kiddo, I think that's a very good idea."

She hung her head and poured more pretend refills. He couldn't stop thinking about that tiara and those costumes she always wore. He felt so damn helpless.

He'd been doing some nosing around on the internet about kids and trauma and had stumbled on an article about therapy dogs being used at schools. He wondered if he should run that idea by Megan now rather than later. Or would she think he was intruding?

As he looked into Evie's green eyes that carried far too many burdens and fears for one so young, he could understand Megan's need to protect her daughter.

Evie's nose scrunched, making her look so much like a mini-Megan. "I can't drive. And if I tell my mommy what I wanna do it will ruin the surprise."

"Are you asking for my help to surprise your mother?"

"Would you?" Her eyes went wide and hopeful. "Please?"

"Can do. In fact, I have an idea." He held out his hand. "If you pass me your iPad we can order shoes online now. Together we can buy lots of shoes."

"You're gonna buy some too? I like that." She sprinted to the sofa and jumped up beside him.

Was she going to hug him? He braced himself.

She rocked back on her heels, her forehead furrowed and worried. "I had two more coins but I bought a sucker. My mommy wouldn't have bought herself a sucker. I should have gotten somethin' for her instead."

He tugged one of her crooked pigtails. "Maybe

we could get something for your mommy while we buy those shoes."

"Like flowers or candy. Mommy likes chocolate—and recycling." She grabbed her iPad off the end table.

He reached for the tablet. "Chocolate and a new recycling bin for your mom."

"Yay!" She wrapped her arms around his neck and squeezed tight. "You're a good boy, Mr. Whit."

God, the little minx was well on her way to wrapping him around her little finger.

On her way?

Too late.

The sense of being watched drew his gaze across the room. Megan stood in the archway between the living room and dining area, holding Tallulah in her arms. Her green eyes glinted with tears. She'd told him she was wary and she had every reason to be given her past. He needed to prove to her he could change, that he was a man worthy of a chance. He didn't know where they were going yet, but he damn well knew he couldn't walk away without digging deeper. Trying harder.

He patted Evie's back and looked at her mom. "Megan, I have an important question to ask."

She blinked in surprise while Evie spun around in her angel dress, humming a tune from the show that had just been on TV.

Megan sniffed and nodded. "Okay. What is it?"

"Can I take my cat home today or do I need to fill out an adoption application at the shelter when you open on Monday?"

# Nine

Megan was so stunned by Whit's request to adopt Tallulah, she almost dropped the cat. She adjusted her hold on the calico and stepped closer to the man who continued to turn her world upside down. "Excuse me? You want to do what?"

"You said Tallulah's better now." He stepped closer to stroke the cat, his knuckles grazing Megan's breasts. "So I thought I could take her home, like you asked me."

She eyed him suspiciously. "Are you doing this just to impress me? Because if so, that's the wrong reason to adopt an animal. A pet is a life-long commitment. If we...break up," the words lodged in her throat for an instant, "you still need to be committed to keeping and loving Tallulah."

He nodded solemnly. "I understand that. We may disagree on a lot of things, but I would never walk out on a commitment. That's why I didn't keep her the first day. I wasn't sure I could care for her the way she deserves. I'm certain now that I can."

Was he talking in some kind of code? Adding layers to his words? Talk of the future made her jittery when she was barely hanging on in the present. "Okay then. When would you like to take Tallulah?"

"I'll need to get supplies for her." He scratched his head. "I'll stop by the pet store on my way home. They'll let me bring her inside, right? I know I'm not supposed to leave an animal in the car."

She stifled a smile. He really was trying. "How about this, Whit? Let me gather some supplies to get you through the night and then you can shop at your leisure tomorrow for the things she'll need. I've got a flyer on file I can email you. We give it to all adopters."

"Thanks. I appreciate that." He leaned in and whispered in her ear, the warm rumble of his voice so close that it incited a nice kind of shiver. "Will Evie be upset to see Tallulah go?"

Megan rested a hand on her daughter's hair, no easy feat as she maneuvered around the halo and tiara. "She understands Tallulah isn't ours. Don't you, sweetie?"

Evie nodded. "Me and Mommy are rescuers. We find good homes for kitties and puppies. Tallulah is Mr. Whit's cat. I'll go get her bed and stuff." She looked up at Whit. "You won't forget about the shoes?"

He knelt down to look Evie in the eyes. "I won't forget. I promise." He tugged a pigtail. "And I always keep my promises."

"Good deal. Thanks." Evie kissed him on the cheek then sprinted to the laundry room where the kitty supplies were kept.

Megan drew in a shaky breath. Seeing flashes of how good life could be with Whit around was tougher than she thought.

He looked at the tiny pink cup in his hand and shrugged sheepishly before setting it down on the coffee table. "About Tallulah—you're not going to call me out on all the BS reasons I gave you about why I couldn't keep a cat in the first place?"

She had questions, but not so much about the cat and certainly not right now with Evie a room away. "I don't believe in saying 'I told you so.'"

"Good to know. I hope there's a lot of information on that list. I've never taken care of an animal on my own before." His eyebrows pinched together and he stuffed his hands in his pockets as if having second thoughts. "I wouldn't want to screw this up."

"I'll be happy to give you our adoption briefing." She held back a smile since she didn't want to hurt his feelings. She truly was touched by his concern. If only more people were this careful. "The most important thing for her now is to get lots of TLC while she bonds with you. So, are you cool with letting her sleep in your lap while you watch ball games?"

"I think I can handle that." He rocked back on his boot heels.

"Sounds good." She rubbed her cheek against Tallulah's dark furry head before passing over the cat. "Let me go dig up an extra scratching post for her to use at your house."

"Would you like to come to dinner at my house tomorrow night?" Whit secured the cat in one arm so he could scratch her under the neck with his other hand. "You can give me that briefing and check on Tallulah."

He was asking her to take a big step. Another meal together. Spending time in his home and in his life. But no matter how nervous those ideas made her—and they still did—she couldn't deny the warm hopefulness that sparked to life insider her either.

Despite the risk, she wanted to try.

The next evening, Whit stepped into his house with Megan and it felt so damn right to have her here it shook the ground under him. She was becoming more and more a part of his life with each day that passed.

Last night's hot dogs with mac and cheese had

tasted a helluva lot better than any of his catered dinners. But then he knew that was due to the people at the table with him. Then he'd taken his cat home. And holy hell, it still surprised him that he'd decided to get a pet. Except it felt right. Still did. His house didn't feel so damn empty with the cat checking out his furniture and deciding which places were worthy of her. Tallulah had sniffed out every corner and seemed to approve of his leather ottoman in the living room. His bed had gotten cat props too; Tallulah had curled up on the pillow next to his head as if she'd been sleeping at his place every night.

He'd actually had a good time using his lunch break to pick up cat gear and drop it off at his house. The calico had leaped off the ottoman in full attack mode when he tossed her a feather squeak toy and before he knew it, he'd spent an extra twenty minutes watching her chase a cat-nip ball and wrestle a fur mouse.

But by the time dinner rolled around he'd been damn near starving. He and Megan had decided to have supper at her house again, then her neighbor would watch Evie after the child went to sleep.

He'd asked Megan to come to his house for dessert. He hadn't wanted to leave his cat alone any longer. Megan's smile told him he'd said the right thing.

She kicked off her shoes and lined them up by the door. "I can't believe you really ordered all those shoes with Evie."

"She's got her mother's entrepreneurial spirit. You've done a good job with her." He slipped an arm around her waist.

"Motherhood is the most important job I've ever had."

"Your commitment shows." His parents had vowed they loved him but they hadn't been big on teaching moral responsibility.

"How's Tallulah?"

"Come say hello to her and see for yourself." He guided her to his study where he'd closed Tallulah in for the evening. The space had a sunroom too, where he'd set up her litter box and food. "I put her in here for the day while she gets acclimated. I thought she would enjoy the sunshine through all the windows. I did some reading on the internet last night on cat care."

He pushed open the double mahogany doors and Megan gasped. She pointed at the six-foot scratching post he'd bought, complete with different levels and cubbies for climbing and snoozing.

"Oh, my God, Whit." She walked to the carpeted and tiered post he'd parked between two leather wingback chairs and reached into a cubby to pet Tallulah. "You obviously went shopping too."

He hefted his cat out and leaned back on the dark wood desk, scratching Tallulah's ears the way she liked. "I just stopped by the pet store on my lunch break and picked up a few essentials."

"A scratching post the size of an oak tree is an essential?"

"It looked cool? What can I say?" He was planning to talk to his contractor buddy Aaron about ordering mini solarium windows for Tallulah to hang out in.

"I wish all our animals could land this well." She dusted cat hair off his suit jacket.

"She needs something to keep her occupied

while I'm at work." Tallulah purred like a freight train in his ear. "And I read online that if I want to save my furniture from her claws, she has to have an appropriate outlet for scratching at home."

Megan had perched on the arm of a wingback. The warmth in her eyes told him he was saying all the right things.

"I also read—" He stopped when the realization hit him. "You already know all of this."

"But it's nice hearing you're excited about having her. Not just in your house but in your life."

And he had to admit, it surprised him too. "I always thought I would be a dog person."

"It doesn't make you any less macho."

"Thanks. I'm not concerned with proving my masculinity."

"Hmm, I have to admit, your confidence about being tender with the cat is very appealing." She trailed a lone finger down his arm in a touch as enticing as any full-on stroke. "If you want a dog though, I'm more than happy to help you find the perfect one for your lifestyle."

One step at a time. "Tallulah needs time to adjust to her new home first."

"Spoken like a natural pet owner. That's really nice to hear." She flicked a cat toy dangling from one of the levels of the scratching post. "Although if you bought Tallulah this, I wonder what you would buy for a dog."

His mind churned with possibilities, like one of those agility courses the Cattleman's Club was working on for the shelter. "I bought one of those climbing trees for Safe Haven too."

"Truly?" she squealed, giving him an enthusiastic kiss with the cat squirming between them. "You do know me better than I gave you credit for."

He tucked Tallulah back into one of the cubbies attached to the climbing post. "You'll even find bottles and paper in the recycling. Will that get me another kiss?"

She laughed and looped her arms around his neck, kissing him again, nothing standing between them now but too many clothes. Her mouth on his felt familiar and new all at once. He knew so much about her, yet there was still so much more of her to explore. And he had a plan in mind for the next few hours to discover more about what pleased her.

Ending the kiss, he angled away while unfastening the clasp holding back her hair. "I'm learning fast that the way to your heart is less traditional than a bouquet of flowers."

She shook her hair free in a silky, wavy cloud around her shoulders and his hands. "Oh, I should share some of the catnip you gave me with Tallulah."

"I have some of my own." He slid an arm around her waist. All day, he'd been fantasizing about showing her his favorite part of the house. "Come with me. There's a part of my home you haven't seen yet."

She eyed him curiously. "I'm intrigued. Lead on."

He steered her into the hall again, toward the back of the house. "This way."

She tucked herself against his side. "Thank you again for helping Evie with the shoe donation drive."

"We shopped for some new video games too."

She stiffened and her footsteps slowed. "I have to approve all of her new games."

"Uh, sure," he said, wishing he'd thought of that himself. But he didn't have nieces or nephews. "Kids are new territory to me too, like the pets. Except I can't exactly shut a kid in a room with a climbing tree and a bowl of food."

"Not unless you want to end up in jail," she said with a laugh in her voice that let him know she wasn't angry with him. "I know you meant well. I just need for you to consult me on anything having to do with Evie."

"Sure, of course." He pushed open the back door into his landscaped yard. "For what it's worth, they were all labeled for her age group and I know the video game developer."

Walking beside him along the flagstone path, she glanced up at him, a hint of frustration in her eyes. "Not all video games are educational."

"You're right, and I do hear you." He guided her toward the left, under an ivy-covered arch. That led to a cluster of trees in the very back of his property. "I'll be more careful about consulting you when it comes to anything with Evie."

"I'm sorry for being prickly." She slid her arm under his suit coat and around his waist. "This is new territory for me too."

"You haven't dated anyone since you had Evie?" Where the hell had that question come from and why was her answer so important?

"In case you haven't noticed, there isn't much spare time in my life between my job and my daughter."

"No one at all?" He stopped at the concrete steps leading into his greenhouse, tucked away in the privacy of a circle of trees.

She took his lapels in her hands. "You're my first venture back into dating since Evie was born."

"I don't want to be your rebound guy." And he meant that. He'd already accepted that he wanted more than a short-term affair with her.

"It's been nearly five years since Evie's biological father walked out of our lives. I'm far past the rebound zone, don't you think?"

Five years? The bastard had walked out before Evie was even born? Whit had heard the jerk wasn't a part of Megan's life, but this was even worse than he'd thought. He let that information roll over him again now that he had a better feel for how much commitment and effort it took to raise a child. He knew logically, of course. But his admiration for how hard Megan had worked grew even more. For that matter, he understood a little better just how tough it must have been for her to let go of that control.

She smoothed his lapels back in place and turned to the greenhouse. "What do we have here?"

He thought about pushing the discussion further, then reconsidered. Better to take his time so he didn't spook her. And luckily for both of them, taking their time had deliciously sensual implications tonight. "Through this door, we have our dessert."

More than a little intrigued, Megan opened the greenhouse door and peered inside the dimly lit building. Warmth and humidity wafted out, carrying a verdant scent of lush life. She stepped inside, expecting some fancy garden typical of the rich and famous. But instead, she found a more practical space, filled with tomato plants and tiered racks of marked herbs, potted trees lining the center of the aisle to give room for their branches to spread. Curiosity drew her in deeper and deeper.

She reached up to tap lemons, limes and even an orange. "This is incredible."

"Glad you like it. The catnip is a recent addition, over that way." He pointed toward the back right corner.

She came around a tree and found a two-seat wrought-iron table set up with plates, water glasses and in the center…a fondue pot? Whit reached past her to turn up the flame.

"Chocolate sauce?" she asked.

"There's a pear tree that's producing, thanks to the climate control in here. When Evie told me you like chocolate, it all came together." He plucked a pear from a branch. "Why the suspicious look?"

"I'm trying to figure out why you're going to so much trouble to win me over?"

"You're worth it." He set the pear on a stone

pottery plate and sliced through it with a paring knife.

"I'm appreciative, but why me when you could expend far less effort for any number of women around here?"

"I don't want them." He swirled the piece of fruit through the chocolate. "Just you." He offered her the dripping slice.

She bit into the end, the sweet fresh pear and gooey chocolate sending her taste buds into a flavor orgasm. She sank into the chair. "Okay, totally amazing," she said, reaching for another slice. "And I'm totally surprised."

"How so?" he sat across from her, their knees bumping under the small table.

"Well," she said, swirling the slice in the chocolate and stroking her toes along his ankle. "I wouldn't have expected you to be so…thrifty."

"I think I was just insulted."

"You're wealthy. Filthy-rich wealthy."

He resisted the impulse to get defensive and forced himself to answer logically. "That doesn't mean I'm wasteful. I've worked damn hard to get to where I am, but there are plenty of people who work just as hard for a lot less, like my mom did. I recognize that there was luck that partnered up with my work ethic."

"Well, your gardener has really outdone himself here." She picked up one of the heavy silver spoons laid out in the fondue display and swirled it through the sauce.

"The hits just keep coming." He laughed. "I don't have a gardener." He popped a slice of fruit in his mouth.

She dropped the spoon in surprise. "You tend all of this yourself?"

Her gaze roamed the neat rows of tomato plants again. The bins of gardening tools and the bags full of potting soil tucked under the plant shelves affirmed that all this work had been done right here. He hadn't just grabbed a bunch of plants from a nursery to decorate his greenhouse. What a lot of work. And patience. She remembered all the times she'd mentally accused him of not caring about the environment and felt a pang of guilt.

"Having money doesn't mean I should stop taking care of things myself." He held up a hand.

"The catering service is a survival thing. I may have a green thumb, but my skills in the kitchen suck. It was less expensive to hire out than to continue throwing away food. Makes economic sense."

"But you don't have to pinch pennies." So much about this man was different than what she'd assumed for the past three years. She hadn't expected him to be so generous and thoughtful, and now to find this "green" side to him? Her head was reeling.

"I grew up in a feast-or-famine kind of childhood. When my dad had a job, we lived well, really well." He tugged an orange from a low-hanging branch and began peeling the ripe fruit. "And then he inevitably got fired and we skipped town, chasing a fresh start. At one point we lived in an RV for about eight months. Even at ten years old, I knew if we'd lived more frugally at the place prior, we would have had enough to carry us through the lean times."

Her heart ached for that little boy with so much upheaval in his life. "How is it that's never shown up in your official bio—or at least the grapevine gossip?"

"My life story is no one's business," he said with the brash confidence she'd seen so often in the past.

Now she saw that confidence with new eyes, saw the man who'd taken adversity and let it drive him to success. She couldn't help but respect that.

She scooped the peels into her hand. "A thrifty woman like myself would recycle this into pot-pourri."

"Hmm, I'm beginning to see merits in your recycling drive." He brought an orange slice to her mouth.

She held it in her teeth, tugging his tie until he leaned across the table to share the bite with her. The fruit burst in her mouth just as their lips met. His eyes held hers as they both ate and watched each other. He kissed a dribble of juice off her chin.

She loosened his tie. "You're a naughty man."

"Lady, I haven't even gotten started yet." He sank back in his seat again, yanking his tie the rest of the way off.

The night outside and the steamed windows inside provided more than enough privacy. It also helped that the greenhouse was tucked away in a cluster of pine trees. They were alone. Truly alone.

Megan's body came alive with anticipation and possibility.

This humid greenhouse was like a tropical retreat in the middle of their everyday small town. What a gift to have such a lush hideaway from the world nestled right here in Whit's backyard.

Standing, he draped his tie over a branch and shrugged out of his coat. She couldn't look away, wondering how far he would go. He flung his coat over the back of his chair and the swoosh of it landing snapped something inside her.

Without taking her eyes off him, she tugged her polo shirt from work over her head. His eyes widened in appreciation and then she lost track of who got undressed faster. She just knew somehow her bra had landed alongside his tie on the orange tree.

She would never again be able to eat an orange without tingling all over.

Whit reached behind a stack of bags full of soil and pulled out a quilt. He'd clearly thought this through and prepared. He shook it on the ground beside the table and took her hand in his. She stepped into his arms and savored the feel of masculine skin against her bare flesh. The rasp of bristle and muscle. A hum of pleasure buzzed through her, melting her as he lowered her onto the blanket.

She trailed her fingers along his shoulders. "This is the most perfect night. You're an ingenious man."

"You inspire me." He pulled an orange slice from the table and held the piece of fruit over her stomach with slow deliberation.

Delicious anticipation shivered through her a second before he squeezed the juice onto her one sweetly torturous drip a time.

"Whit," she gasped just as he dipped his head to sip away each drop.

He glanced up the length of her. "Should I stop?" he asked, kissing his way upward.

Her elbows gave way and she sank back. He snagged the rest of the orange from the iron table and drizzled more juice along one breast, his mouth soon following. She arched up into his caress and gave her hands free rein to enjoy this intriguing, sexy man who'd found his way into her life.

She let herself be swept away in sensations and desire. He was an intuitive lover, lingering when she sighed, in tune to the cues of her least sound or movement. His mouth skimmed lower and lower still until her knees parted and…yes… he sipped and licked, nuzzling at the bundle of nerves drawing tighter. He coaxed her pleasure closer and closer to the edge of completion.

For so long she'd been alone, and while she'd told herself she didn't need more in her life, right now she knew that was a lie. She needed this. This man.

The thought sent a bolt of ecstasy through her. Her fingers gripped his shoulders and dug in to let him know just how much she needed him to stay with her for every wave of pleasure. And he did, as each wave rippled through her.

Her arms fell to her sides as she breathed in ragged gasps, her mind still in a fog. But even in her afterglow haze, need already built inside her again.

Soon, the goal of having Whit reach those heights with her had her reaching for another orange.

# Ten

Tucking Megan to his side, Whit trailed his fingers up and down her arm, making the most of their last minutes together tonight. He understood she had to be home soon to relieve the sitter, but he wanted more time with Megan. He'd never dated a single mother before.

More importantly, he'd never been with anyone who captivated him the way she did, dressed or undressed. Although right now he was enjoying the hell out of the undressed Megan. Her silky hair teased along his arm in a fan of red. He'd explored every inch of her soft, pale skin.

He kissed a smudge of chocolate off her nose.

Chocolate and oranges would long be his favorite flavors. He'd discovered a lot about her this evening, and intended to make the most of the time they had left before she sent the sitter home at midnight. "Penny for your thoughts."

Megan rubbed her foot along his calf. "Why do you have a greenhouse full of fruits and vegetables if you order your food catered?"

He propped up on one elbow and gestured at the plants on either side. "There's a theme here, if you look closer," he said, surprised at her question but glad to have a chance to extend the evening. "Fresh fruits and vegetables for a salad or salsa. I may not be able to cook, but I can chop. Plus, free tomatoes are a great way to make friends with your neighbors."

"Just being neighborly?" she pressed. "I think there's more to your answer than that."

"Believe it or not, I like roots." If he wanted more from her, he would need to give more of himself. "I moved around so much as a kid, this place reminds me I'm here to stay."

One of those happy-sad smiles played on her

lips, which were still plump from kissing. "You break my heart sometimes."

"How so?" He tensed. He didn't want her pity. Part of him wanted to pull back, but that would mean letting her go. And with her hands sketching lazy circles all over him, staying put seemed a better option.

"With those images of you as a kid longing for a home." One of her hands slid up to cradle his face.

"You're a nurturer." He kissed her palm.

"You're a builder and tender too, you know." She gestured to the greenhouse. "You just have to learn to see that in yourself."

Okay, enough of this kind of talk. It was one thing to share parts of their past. It was another altogether to submit to a cranial root canal. "This conversation is getting entirely too serious."

"Then why did you bring me out here and show me this part of your life?"

Why had he? Every time he got close to that answer, he mentally flinched away as if he were getting too close to a flame. He settled on the easy answer. "Because I had been fantasizing about making love to you out here, about tasting the fruit on your skin."

She paused and he could see in her eyes she wasn't buying into his dismissal of her assessment. Then she nodded as if conceding to give him space on the issue and arched up to nibble his bottom lip. "You taste mighty delicious yourself."

"I've developed a new appreciation for fondue."

She flicked her tongue along his chin before pressing her mouth to his collar bone, then settling back into his arms. "I appreciate the dessert and the thought that went into arranging such an amazing evening, and all you've done for Evie and for the shelter as well."

"I would like to pamper you every day if you would let me." He massaged along one of her narrow shoulders, then down her back, skimming along her curves and around her hip where he knew her tattoo trailed across her skin. He could get so used to this. "The way I see it, you don't get much time to relax between work and being a mom."

"I love my daughter and my job. That's always

been enough." Yet as she said that, her eyes fluttered closed and she melted against him.

"That doesn't mean you can't have recreation."

"Is that what you are?" She tipped her face to look at him. "My recreation?"

"I'm just trying to be a help. We all need a break every now and again, right?" He couldn't hold back the burning question any longer. "Where does Evie's father live?"

Her body went rigid under his touch and she rolled away, sitting up and gathering her clothes. "Not here. He's not a part of her life and chances are he never will be."

"But he knows about her."

"Of course," she answered indignantly, tugging on her panties, then her bra. "I would never keep that a secret. The minute he found out, he cut ties and ran."

The bastard. Whit wanted to find the guy and pummel him for the pain he'd caused Megan and her amazing daughter.

"He doesn't pay child support, does he?" Whit tugged on his suit pants.

She shrugged and pulled on her shirt. "He

snowed me. Completely. Last I heard he was in the Keys heading for the Bahamas."

"Hey." Whit cradled her face in his hands. "It's not your fault he's a loser. He missed out on an amazing family." Whit's own father may not have been much of a provider but at least he'd been there.

"My fault or not," she gripped his wrists and stared straight into his eyes, "Evie will grow up knowing her father didn't want her and there's nothing I can do to change that."

She pulled away to slip on her khakis, her rigid back telling him she was holding on by a thread while rebuilding defenses he'd apparently blasted with one simple question.

Whit could see he didn't just need to be careful for Evie's sake. Megan was every bit as wounded by the past as her daughter. She just didn't wear the costumes.

And now he prayed like hell his idea to help with Evie wouldn't backfire.

"What's the matter with you?"

Beth's question cut through Megan's fog as she

picked at her lunch salad the next day. Evie had taken her lunch box and joined Miss Abigail at the front desk.

Megan sagged back in her office chair, the squeak in the old seat mixing with the muffled sound of a couple of dogs in the play yard. The kennel runs were quieter today than usual thanks to some new calming CDs brought in by one of the volunteers. If only that music could help calm her spinning thoughts.

Even the salad reminded her of Whit's greenhouse and how hard he was trying on her behalf. Yet she couldn't shake the jittery feeling that things would fall apart, and the closer she let herself get to him, the worse the breakup would hurt.

Tossing aside her fork, Megan reached for her water instead, staring at the photo on her desk of beach day in Galveston when Evie was two. She'd scrimped and saved for that trip, convinced she needed to start making special memories with her toddler. "I'm just preoccupied."

"Because of Whit?" Beth unpacked her navy blue lunch sack that could have passed for a purse. "How did it go last night?"

"Did you know he has this massive greenhouse where he grows fresh fruits and veggies?"

Beth's eyebrows shot up. "No, I didn't know. And you think he would have told me since I have an organic farm. We could have shared clippings—" She stopped. "Wait. This is about you."

Megan tapped the catnip plant. "He brought this for the kitties. And he's rolling out all the stops romancing me and I have to admit, he seems so sincere."

"Seems?" Beth absently thumbed her engagement ring, spinning it around on her finger.

Admitting her insecurities, even to her close friend, was tough for Megan. But God, if she didn't work through this and she blew it with Whit without even trying… "I don't trust my instincts when it comes to men. And he's known for being ruthless."

"In the work world," Beth pointed out. "That's different."

"Is it?"

"He adores Evie. He's not faking that. Evie would sense that a mile off." The natural blonde beauty smiled. "Remember that banker guy who pretended to be in the market for a dog so he could hit on you about six months ago? Evie made a point of getting peanut butter and jelly on his ties so you would see him freak out over kid germs."

Megan laughed at the memory. "She's a great little bodyguard." But even that thought was sobering in light of her daughter's fears since the storm. "Can I afford to let Evie grow any more attached to Whit when I'm not sure where the relationship is headed?"

"Unless you intend to spend your life alone, at some point you have to trust again," Beth said with undeniable reason.

"I could wait until Evie's eighteen." Except after last night's sex, fourteen years felt like an eternity.

Her friend stayed diplomatically silent and bit into an apple.

The noise level in the lobby grew. New voices and a squeal from Evie drew Megan's attention away from her pity party, thank heaven, because talking was just making her feel worse today.

She rolled back her chair and stood. "Beth, I should see what's going on out there."

She stepped into the lobby, her eyes drawn immediately to Whit. What was he doing here in the middle of the workday? Then she noticed Evie petting a golden retriever. Megan's instincts went on alert at the thought of her daughter petting a possible stray with an unknown vaccination history. Except then she saw the dog was wearing a "service dog" vest. What did all of this have to do with Whit's arrival?

He turned to face her—and he wasn't alone. A sleekly pretty woman with dark hair stood at his side. Jealousy nipped. Hard.

Megan smiled tightly and knelt beside her daughter. "Sweetie, that vest means this is a working dog. We don't touch dogs with this special vest."

Her daughter—dressed as a Ninja Turtle today—grinned. "I asked. She said it was okay and Mr. Whit said it was okay. He brought the dog for my preschool class."

Megan glanced up at him, confused. "What's going on?"

Whit set his Stetson on the receptionist's desk. "I talked to the day-care director about bringing in a therapy dog for the kids given all they went through with the tornado. The local school psychologist recommended this group in Dallas and contacted the other parents to clear it. I said I would check with you to save her a call, and well, here we are. The dog handler said she's even interested in evaluating the dogs here for training."

Introductions were made in a blur and the next thing she knew her wonderfully intuitive friend Beth was offering to walk the dog handler—Zoe Baker—back to the play yard.

Megan's head was spinning in surprise. Of course it was a great idea, but having someone take over decisions for her daughter so totally felt…alien. But there wasn't much she could say since he'd gone straight to the school and she didn't want to cause a scene that would upset Evie.

Still, she ducked her head and said, "Could we talk for a minute. Alone."

Miss Abigail knelt beside Evie. "Would you

like to come with me to play with the cats? Your mom told me a new litter of kittens was just brought in."

Evie skipped alongside Abigail with a new spring in her step Megan hadn't seen in a month.

Whit swept his hat off the desk and followed Megan to her office. "I meant this to be a surprise, to show you I care about you and Evie, that I respect your work with animals."

"Okay," she said cautiously, "but why not consult me? This is my child. And animals are my area of expertise."

He scratched his head, wincing. "You're right. I should have. I was thinking about Evie's fear of going back to school and then I saw this article about the group in Dallas and I got caught up in the moment wanting to surprise you. Like with the catnip."

"This is a much bigger deal than catnip."

She couldn't help but feel defensive. "I don't want to push her before she's ready."

"Hey," he took her shoulders in his hands, "I'm not questioning your parenting. Thinking of her made me wonder about the other kids.

So I spoke with some of the dads at the Cattleman's Club and asked if their kids were having trouble this past month. This is for all of them. Not just Evie."

"You talked to the other parents…about their children?" Her lips went tight, anger nipping all over again.

But she couldn't help but remember how carefully he'd studied the instructions for taking care of Tallulah. Thinking about that kind of thoughtfulness applied to her daughter touched her. "Which other children?"

"Sheriff Battle said every time his son hears a train he thinks the tornado's coming back." He turned his hat around and around in his hands. "When I saw that article about therapy dogs going into nursing homes and schools, it got me thinking. Ms. Baker uses shelter dogs, which I knew would be appealing to you. I even learned there's a difference between service dogs, therapy dogs and emotional support dogs. Anyhow, what do you think? Aside from the fact I've been pushy, when I should have consulted you."

"I actually think that's a great idea. I'm kicking myself for not thinking of it." She sagged back against the edge of her desk. "You sure acted on this quickly."

"You've had your hands full. And I figured why wait. The day-care staff is expecting us this afternoon. I'm hoping Evie will be excited to take the dog to show off to her friends."

"I still wish you'd consulted me. We talked about this yesterday."

He flinched. "Guilty as charged and I truly am sorry. It seemed like a good surprise in my head. Would you have said no if I told you?"

Sighing, she conceded, "Of course not."

But that wasn't the point.

He scratched the back of his neck. "My buddies thought it was funny as hell that I was asking about kid stuff so word got around fast. The press is involved now too, planning to cover it. I figured it would be a good chance to talk about shelter dogs and how full your rescue is."

And he'd done all this for her when she'd given so little of herself in return. She'd just held back and questioned and worried. "You're really going all out to win me over."

"Busted." He slid his arms around her waist. "I want to be with you."

She toyed with his tie and knew he wouldn't give a damn if Evie painted it with jelly. "I'm still the same pain-in-the-butt person who's fighting with you over what parts of Royal you choose to develop."

"And I'm still the same guy who's going to argue there's a way around things."

"We're going to argue," she said with certainty.

"At least you'll be talking to me rather than ignoring me."

"Hey," she tugged his tie, "you ignored me too."

He tugged her loose ponytail in return. "I gave you space when it looked like you were going to cause a scene."

Before she could launch a retort, he kissed her silent, and this man knew how to kiss. Her arms slid around his neck and she knew without question he was a good man who would try like hell for her.

Which was going to make this hurt so much worse if it didn't work out.

Whit was mighty damn pleased with how the therapy dog issue had shaken down.

He stood in the back of the Little Tots Daycare classroom with Megan while all the kids sat in a circle on a rug. The town had done an amazing job at getting the facility functional quickly so the children could get back into a regular routine, the kind of reassurance they needed after such a frightening event.

Their teacher was reading them a book about tornadoes. The golden retriever was calm, but alert, carefully moving from child to child as if knowing which one was most in need of comfort, whether with a simple touch of his paw or resting his head on a knee, or just letting a dozen little hands burrow in his fur.

As the teacher closed the book, she looked up at her students. "What do you think about the story we just read?"

Beside Evie, a little girl with glasses admitted, "I was scared."

"Not me," said the boy in tiny cowboy boots sitting on the other side of Evie.

"Yes, you were," the girl with glasses retorted. "You were crying. I saw you wipe boogers on your sleeve."

Evie raised her hand until the teacher called on her. "I was scared," Evie said. "I told my mom I held Caitlyn's hand 'cause she was scared. But it was really me. I was the fraidy cat."

The retriever belly crawled over to Evie and rested his head on her leg. Evie rubbed the dog's ears, her eyes wide and watery.

The teacher leaned forward in her rocking chair. "We were all afraid that day. That's why we have the drills. So we know what to do in an emergency."

Evie kept stroking the dog and talking. "What if another tora-na-do comes to our school? What if it hurts Mommy's car again, 'cept it gets Mommy too?"

Megan started to move forward, but Whit rested a hand on her arm. It was hard as hell for him to hear the little imp's fears too, but she was talking. Thank God, she was talking. Megan's hand slid into his and held on.

The teacher angled forward, giving all the right grown-up answers that Evie took in with wide eyes, both her hands buried in the dog's fur.

Evie kept talking, but she smiled periodically. Something that didn't happen often.

Megan's chin trembled. "This is so incredible to watch," she whispered.

"I wouldn't have even thought twice about the article if not for you." He ducked his head to keep their voices low so as not to disturb the class. "You do a good job educating about your work at the shelter."

"Thank you." Her cheeks flushed a pretty pink.

"I knew about service dogs for the disabled and I'd heard there were studies showing that owning a pet lowers blood pressure." He scanned the group of little ones up front with the dog. "But this is a whole new world." In more ways than one.

"I think of it all as the balance of nature."

"That makes sense."

"Taking care of our resources." She looked up at him pointedly.

"Hey, I've started recycling water bottles and cans because of you."

She clapped a hand to her chest. "Be still my heart."

"Are you making fun of me?" He raised an eyebrow. "I happen to think that was a very romantic gesture on my part."

"It is sweet. But you would be wise to remember, sometimes I don't have much of a sense of humor when it comes to things like this. You just caught me on a good day."

"Fair enough." He had a feeling there was a lot more to learn about Megan before he could banish the wary look that still lurked in her green eyes. "I will keep that in mind."

He glanced at his watch, and damn, he was running late. When he woke up this morning, he hadn't thought there was a chance in hell he could get through the day of Craig's memorial service without a bottle by his side. But Megan and Evie had given him a welcome distraction. They were good for him.

"Do you have a meeting?" she asked.

"I need to go home to change and get some things together for Craig's memorial service."

She pressed a trembling hand to her mouth. "Oh God, Whit, I'm so sorry. How selfish of me not to think about how difficult today is for you." She touched his shoulder lightly. "What can I do?"

"This helped keep my mind off things."

"I'll meet you at the church."

"You don't have to—"

"I want to be there for you."

He brushed his hand along her back, which was as much contact as would be appropriate here in a classroom full of kids. But he knew how tough it was for Megan to spend time away from her daughter and appreciated her being there for him. "I'll see you tonight."

This wasn't a day when he could feel joyful by any means, but suddenly the weight didn't seem as heavy.

Since her parents' death, Megan had avoided funerals and memorial services, but she'd wanted to be here for Whit. As she stood in the church vestibule with Whit after the service, she was relieved it was over, and certain that attending had been absolutely the right decision.

It had been emotional experience for everyone. Not just mourning their friend, but also remembering that fateful day all their lives had been forever changed so quickly. Paige Richardson's husband was taken from her in an instant…. A thought that had Megan reaching for Whit's hand.

Whit's words about his friend had brought tears to her eyes, reaffirming how important it was to be here for him. He was trying so hard and there was danger in a relationship that was too one-sided. It wasn't fair to him.

At least the service had been in the evening so she wouldn't be spending as much time away from Evie. Her daughter had been excited talking about going to preschool tomorrow. She'd chattered about her friends and all the fun activities coming up for December.

Megan stood silently at Whit's side while he gave his condolences to Craig Richardson's widow Paige and his twin brother Colby, who'd returned to town from his home in Dallas.

Everyone was making small talk, doing their best to hold it together. Then Whit took her elbow and guided her outside, shouldering through the crowd and into the chilly night full of stars. In the dark, the scars from the storm didn't show. It was almost if it never happened. Except tonight reminded her too well it had.

She tucked her arm in his. "Are you okay?"

"Hanging in there. It's hard to believe he's been gone for over a month." Whit sighed, cricking his neck to the side as they walked to his truck.

"Did I hear right that R&N Builders is helping out with the reconstruction?" Colby Richardson and Whit's friend Aaron Nichols were partners in the business.

"You did. Colby has offered all the services of his very successful company to help," Whit confirmed, although his forehead was still furrowed over what should have been a good piece of news.

"I'm sure you'll be glad to have more time with your friends, especially now."

"Hmm."

She squeezed his arm as they walked. "Something's bothering you?"

"The whole evening is just surreal. Especially seeing Colby with Paige."

"Because Colby is Craig's twin?"

He shook his head. "Because Colby and Craig each went out with Paige in high school. There is still a lot of tension between Colby and Paige."

"It must be difficult for her to have him around reminding her of her dead husband."

"Maybe so." He nodded, stopping beside his truck and opening the door for her. "Tonight sure makes a person think hard about what's important."

"That's an understatement." She climbed inside, thinking back to the first time she'd sat inside this vehicle, terrified for her daughter.

He settled behind the wheel without starting the truck. "It meant a lot to me to have you here."

"Of course I was here for you."

He stretched his arm along the seat, his fingers toying with her hair. "I think we both know what we have going is about more than sex."

His words stirred up a flurry of nerves in her

belly. "Are you saying you're thinking about happily ever after and white picket fences?"

"I'm saying you mean something to me." He angled toward her, his eyes intense in the darkness. "And yeah, that scares the hell out of me, but this isn't casual. Not for me."

"Well, it scares the hell out of me to think about letting a man in my life again." As terrified as she was to say the words out loud, tonight had reminded her there were no guarantees in life. She linked her fingers with his. "But it scares me more to think about not trying at all."

# Eleven

Whit couldn't remember being this nervous—and genuinely pumped up—about a Friday night date.

But then he'd never proposed to a woman before.

The diamond solitaire damn near burning a hole in his suit coat pocket, he shifted gears on his Porsche as he drove through Royal with Megan at his side. They weren't hiding out in some tucked away place. He'd chosen a restaurant near his Pine Valley home, where the odds of running into friends were high. Megan had agreed. The whole town knew they were dating. Evie had accepted him into their routine this past week.

And soon, everyone would see the ring on her finger.

Things were moving fast, sure, but during the week since Craig's memorial service, Whit had felt as if he and Megan had lived two lifetimes together. Their lives fit together. More than fit. They were good together and he didn't want to lose that. He'd been searching his whole life for a steady home life to build a family. Megan was the perfect woman for him.

Steering through the night streets, he noted the Christmas lights just beginning to crop up in windows and could see the efforts to rebuild the town starting to bear fruit. There was still a lot of work to be done, but then couldn't that be said about life overall? Everything was a work in progress. And he looked forward to meeting the challenge with Megan at his side.

God, she was gorgeous in a green lace dress, her thick hair swept up into one of those loose kinds of topknots that somehow stayed in place but begged his fingers to set free. She was such an intriguing mix of contrasts. On the one hand, a no-nonsense kind of woman not afraid to get her hands dirty whether she was working with animals or building a compost heap. On the other hand, an elegant woman as comfortable curled up reading her daughter a book as she was dressing up for a five-star evening out. Megan's confidence didn't come from a sense of entitlement or wealth. It came from within. From having tackled life head on and made her way in the world.

He respected that.

Megan trailed her fingers along the window as they drove past the Royal Diner, still closed due to damages from the storm. "Evie and I used to have supper there on days I would work late."

"Amanda will reopen," he said. "It's just going to take a while. I hear she and Nathan took out good insurance on the place. With luck the diner will be even better than ever."

"Like the hospital?" She smoothed a hand over her green lace dress. "I almost feel guilty getting all dressed up to have fun when there are still people dealing with the chaos of the aftermath."

"There's nothing wrong with enjoying yourself. You work hard and deserve a break. I think even the people who are struggling take comfort from seeing life returning to normal around them. It's good to do regular things. Support local businesses." He rested his hand on top of the steering wheel. "I know a perfect diner Evie will love when you two move in with me—I guess I should say, 'What if you and Megan moved in with me?'"

Wait, that wasn't what he'd meant to say. He was going to propose, then ask her to move in while they were engaged. But damn it, the words were already out there, so he held his peace as he stopped at a red light and waited for her response.

"What did you say?" she asked carefully.

"I have plenty of space." The light changed and he accelerated, weighing his words. "It's a gated community, so you two would have more security. And Evie would enjoy the Pine Valley community stables and pool. I'm thinking she could use some jodhpurs. Maybe for Christmas?"

"Maybe," Megan said noncommittally. To the riding clothes or moving in?

He needed to shift into damage control ASAP.

"Is that a no to moving in?" If so, that didn't bode well for his plans to propose.

"You've sprung this on me rather quickly. Can we talk more about it, please?" Her fingers clenched and tangled together in her lap. "I have a lot to consider with Evie. She's only just stopped wearing costumes—thank you again for bringing the therapy dog to her school. You were right about that."

Did that mean she trusted him more? "I did it for all the kids. And for the animals too. I'm glad Ms. Baker was able to take two off your hands."

"You and me both." She twisted in the seat toward him. "I didn't mean to be short about moving in together. You just caught me unaware."

He glanced at her beautiful face, full of worry. "It's okay. Like you said, we can talk more later. We have time."

They had time and he had plans. He knew the right opportunity would present itself for the proposal. And he'd even chosen a gift for her he thought would let her know just how much he cared about her as a person and accepted their differences.

She smiled, and it damn near took his breath away. "Taking our time. I like the sound of that."

Megan had barely tasted a bite of the appetizer, soup, salad or main course. Her mind was still on Whit's surprise suggestion that they live together. Things were moving so fast, she felt as if she was still stuck in the tornado sometimes.

But with each minute that passed, she found herself considering the possibility more seriously.

They were all but spending every waking hour outside of work together. Evie didn't even question his presence. If anything, her daughter questioned when he would arrive. She'd even asked if he could pick her up from day care. He was everything Megan could have hoped for in a man, on so many levels. So much so, it scared her sometimes how well things were going. Maybe that's why she was nervous about moving in together. It was like tempting fate.

The waiter cleared away their dinner plates and brought dessert. "Mr. Daltry," the waiter said, "just as you ordered, our chef made this especially for your celebration. A dark chocolate and orange tart with toasted almonds. I hope it is to your satisfaction."

Orange and chocolate? Surely not a coincidence?

The twinkle in Whit's eyes confirmed he'd intended the treat as a reminder of their time together in the greenhouse.

"I'm sure it will be perfect," Whit answered smoothly. "Please pass along my thanks."

Megan pressed a hand to her mouth to stop a laugh as the waiter left them alone again. "You're wicked."

"Just reminding you of all the wonderful times we can have together in the future." His hand gravitated to his suit coat, smoothing his lapel as he'd done a number of times throughout the dinner.

Was he as nervous as she over this? In a strange way she found it comforting, more of a sign he took this big step seriously.

"About what you said in the car regarding moving in together, I'm still not ready to say yes outright, but I want to think about it. And for me that's huge."

His hand fell away from his jacket and she linked fingers with him.

"Whit, we have something wonderful started. Let's not rush."

"Sure, of course," he agreed, but the tight lines of his mouth indicated that she'd let him down.

Couldn't he see how hard she was trying by letting herself be swept into his world so fast? She thought they'd really made progress. And it wasn't as if she just had herself to consider. A move would be a lot of upheaval for Evie at a time when she was just settling back into school and enjoying herself.

Megan tried to think of a better way to help Whit understand—to ease that tense expression on his face—when a cleared throat from behind him drew her attention upward.

Colby Richardson stood there with his hands shoved in his pockets. His resemblance to his late brother Craig was shocking. The man had a closed-off air emotionally, but that was understandable given what he must be going through. "Sorry to interrupt your dinner, but I wanted to congratulate you."

Megan looked up in confusion. Whit couldn't have already told people of his plans to move in together, could he? Whit stood, as if to quiet the man, which only fueled her concerns—and confusion.

"Thanks, Colby. I appreciate that. Could I treat your table to another round of drinks?" Whit asked, clearly trying to divert him.

"Of course. I see you have a bottle of champagne on its way over. I should leave you both to celebrate your big purchase."

Megan frowned. "Big purchase?"

"Yes," Colby said. "Whit managed quite a coup this week in scooping up the stretch of wetlands on the edge of town."

Her insides chilled faster than that bottle of bubbly in the ice bucket. "You bought up the wetlands?"

"Yes," Whit shuffled his feet, "but it's not exactly what you're thinking."

Colby backed away. "Sorry to have spilled the beans prematurely. I'll just leave the two of you to talk. Good evening."

The clean-cut real estate mogul turned and

made a beeline to his table, leaving Megan alone with Whit again.

She restrained the urge to snap at Whit. He was a businessman, first and foremost. She knew that. She shouldn't be surprised that he'd proceeded as planned. He'd never misled her about who he was.

Still, she couldn't stem the deep well of disappointment pooling in her stomach.

"Megan? Do you want to hear what I have to say?"

She shook her head. "It doesn't matter." She folded her napkin in her lap, wishing she could sweep this disagreement away along with the breadcrumbs. "I understand we're different people. I'm not angry."

It cost her, but she would make peace. Try harder. Damn it, she was trying harder.

"But you're upset with me." Tension threaded through his shoulders, his jaw flexing.

She met his eyes and answered honestly. "Disappointed."

"Megan, our careers are separate. I respect your professionalism and I expect you to respect mine."

"Okay," she answered carefully, "but that doesn't mean I'm going to compromise my principles."

"You're calling me unprincipled?"

She struggled for a way to wind back out of this discussion that was playing out like too many confrontations they'd had over the years. Had the past couple of weeks just been a fluke, with reality now intruding once again? "We've had this disagreement for years. Did you think I was magically going to change because we…"

She couldn't even push the last words free without her voice cracking. She snatched up her water glass, her hand trembling with emotion.

He held her eyes without speaking for what felt like an eternity. Dishes and silverware clanked. The candles flickered between them, the dim chandelier above casting more shadows than light.

Finally, he shook his head. "You've already made up your mind about me. It's clear we have nothing left to say to each other."

How dare he act disillusioned with her? In the span of a couple of weeks, she'd done an about-face on so many of her stances to be with him. She was even willing to overlook this land purchase, as much as it galled her, and accept that they were different.

But now she suspected in spite of all his words to the contrary, he didn't want to be with her after all. Because it wasn't good enough for him that she would compromise on this issue. He needed her to be on his side. Think like him. Cheer on his plan to destroy wetlands she felt passionately about.

Why couldn't they just leave it be? Like so many men she'd seen in the past, he was okay to let their relationship self-destruct. He'd found an out and taken it. The knowledge burned all the way down her throat. She shot up from her chair before she did something humiliating like burst into tears.

Or worse yet, accept anything he said as truth just to stay with him.

Anger and frustration making his blood boil, Whit strode through the restaurant after Megan. He angled past the Richardson family at one table, the sheriff and his wife at another, and barely registered that they spoke to him because his focus was fully on Megan.

He charged past a Christmas tree covered in golden lone stars and white twinkling lights. Whit pushed through the door and stopped beside Megan, who was standing under the restaurant awning. "Megan—"

"The doorman is calling a cab for me." Her arms were crossed tight over her chest as her teeth chattered, her face every bit as chilly as her body language.

He held up a hand to stop the doorman from hailing a taxi. "Damn it, that's not necessary. I brought you here. I'll drive you home."

"That would be awkward." She squeezed her eyes closed and then nodded to the doorman, silently signaling him to flag down a ride. "Please, just let me go. You already made it clear we have nothing left to say to one another."

Her struggle to hold back tears tugged at him. Damn it all, the last thing he wanted was to hurt her. But pride held him back from telling her the truth about that land. He needed her to believe in him. "You're upset. I get that." He took her arm and gently guided her away from the restaurant's main entrance. "But this isn't the place."

She let him steer her a few steps to the side. "The facts won't change if we're in your car."

"The facts?" He bit back a weary sigh. "You don't understand—"

"How about this for facts?" Her arms slid to her side, her hands clenched in tight fists. "You've been buying up land since the tornado. Taking advantage of people's pain. So fine. Tell me how I'm wrong," she finished defiantly.

"Taking advantage?" He searched for the words to make her understand, for the words to keep her in his life. "I've been buying property from people who needed to cut their losses. If I wasn't there to buy from them, they would lose everything rather than walking away with the money to start over. We've discussed this before."

He'd spent his childhood seeing his family's life repossessed. He wasn't lying when he told her he tried to help people in his town as best he could. He swallowed back the past and focused on the present, on Megan.

She shook her head. "And destroying the wet-lands? How is that 'helping' people? Sounds like you're making excuses. You can justify it how-ever you want, but I don't see it the same way."

The sound system hummed with a symphonic version of "Have Yourself a Merry Little Christ-mas," as if mocking him with memories of a holiday spent in a homeless shelter until his dad landed on his feet again. Granted, they had all gotten gifts that year, courtesy of a local church group.

Even if he told her his real reason for buying the wetlands, that wouldn't change who he was. "You're employed by a non-profit organization and get paid a salary. I own a business where people only get paid if I make a profit. That's how life works."

She held up a finger, her hand shaking with restrained emotion. "Don't speak to me like I'm a child. There are plenty of people who make a profit without compromising their values."

"I follow the letter of the law in my business practices." He wasn't like his father, damn it.

"Just because something is legal doesn't mean it's morally right."

Okay, now she was stepping over the line.

"And what makes you the authority on right and wrong? There can be a middle ground if you'll stop being judgmental and—"

Gasping, she backed up a step. "Is that what you think of me? That I'm uptight and judgmental just because I live my life by a moral code that isn't identical to yours?"

He looked into her eyes and didn't see any room for changing her mind. She'd dug in her heels deeply. He recognized the look from the three years he'd known her. These past few weeks had been an anomaly. She wasn't interested in a real relationship with him.

"I think you're just looking for a reason to break it off with me. I think you're so locked onto the past that you're convinced every man is like your dad or Evie's dad. So much so, that you never really gave me a chance. Not three and a half years ago and not now."

"That's not fair," she whispered.

"None of this is." His hand gravitated to the

ring box in his pocket again by habit, but he left it inside. He met her gaze and willed her to see the love in his eyes, to understand how he felt. To trust him.

To trust *in* him.

For an instant, he could have sworn he saw her stance softening and he reached to caress her arm.

The taxi rolled to a stop at the front entrance.

She pulled her hands in tight again, closing herself off from him, from what they could have had together. "Goodnight, Whit. I just…I can't do this."

Looking so damn beautiful that she took his breath away and broke his heart, Megan rushed past him and slid into the cab.

The taxi's taillights disappeared into the night like fading Christmas lights. His big night with Megan was over and he'd botched it from the start. He'd been so busy making plans for them, looking for angles to persuade her and win her over. All the while missing the most important thing of all.

This wasn't about winning a deal like some

business merger. This was about having Megan in his life forever. This was about being in love with her. Somehow, he'd never once used that all-important word and because of that, he'd lost her.

# Twelve

After a sleepless night, Megan took out her frustration by trying to restore order to some part of her world. She grabbed the bottle of disinfectant and moved on to spritz the next cat kennel. Her gloved hands scrubbed with a vengeance.

She'd spent most of the night crying and second-guessing herself. Today was supposed to be a day off. She should have been spending it with Whit. Evie had even asked to go to a friend's house to play, her costumes and fears fading. Which left Megan alone in her too quiet house. So she'd come to the shelter to get her mind off things, but it wasn't working.

Somehow she and Whit had shifted from considering moving in together to broken up in the span of one dinner, and all because of a land purchase.

A land purchase they had been at odds over for months.

She should have seen the signs, but she'd been so blinded by how much she enjoyed being with him. Her eyes watered again. She sniffled and rubbed her wrist under her nose.

Footsteps echoed in the corridor and she blinked faster to clear her eyes—as if that would make any difference given how puffy they were. God, she hoped whoever it was wouldn't stop and talk. She just wanted to clean and clean until she dropped into an exhausted sleep and didn't have to think.

The footsteps stopped right outside the doorway.

"Soooo?" Beth's voice called. "How did your big date with Whit go last night?"

Megan could have diverted an employee or regular volunteer. But there would be no escaping Beth.

Eyes stinging from the sharp scent of bleach, she spoke over her shoulder, keeping her face averted. "The meal was five-star quality."

"Everyone knows the place is great." Beth pulled up alongside her. "It's one of those restaurants where guys take women to propose. Megan? Sweetie? Are you okay?" Beth dipped her head to make eye contact.

Megan flinched and scrubbed harder. "Would you like to help me here? I'm expecting a call from a grant writer any minute." Her words tumbled over each other as she sought to distract. "The guy's going to donate his services to help us put in a proposal to help fund a voucher spay/ neuter program."

Beth grabbed a second bottle of antiseptic spray and tore off some paper towels. "Abigail and I can finish up here. On one condition."

She tucked her head into the steel kennel. "What's that?"

Her friend rested a hand on her shoulder. "Can you take off the glove so I can see the ring?"

Is that what her friend thought? This day just got worse.

Megan knew the moment had come. She couldn't hide anymore. "There's no ring."

She couldn't even begin to think about all that didn't happen between them last night. All her hopes...up in flames.

"Oh. Really? I could have sworn that he planned to..." Genuine confusion was stamped on Beth's face. "I mean..."

Seeing her friend's certainty was bittersweet. "Just because he takes me out to eat doesn't mean he planned to propose."

Beth took Megan by the shoulders gently and turned her. "Those are dark circles under your puffy eyes. Were you crying? Honey, what's wrong?"

Megan sagged back against the empty kennels they used for new cats to get acclimated before going into the free roaming facility. "We had a...really bad argument, and, well, it's over between us."

"No," Beth whispered, "that's not possible."

But it was. She knew that all too well. "I heard about his land grab...the wetlands."

Beth's eyes narrowed. "Who told you that?"

"Colby Richardson. We crossed paths at the restaurant last night."

"What did Whit say when you asked him for his side of things?"

"I said I…I mean, we talked about it." She chewed her bottom lip, thinking back over their argument and trying to remember when things really went off the rails. "He didn't deny it."

Beth nodded, but stayed silent.

Alarms jangled in Megan's mind. "You're trying to say there was a good reason for what he did?"

She thought back over the evening. It had been the perfect setup for a proposal. He'd even asked her to move in on the drive over. He was clearly serious.

Reflecting on how quickly things had spiraled out of control, she started to question why she hadn't asked rather than just assume. At the time it had seemed as if asking would have given him a chance to lie. But now she wondered if she had subliminally sabotaged the evening because deep down, she was afraid to trust any man again. Just as Whit had accused her of doing.

She looked at Beth, guilt stinging over the way she'd jumped to conclusions when Whit had done nothing but try to see and meet her needs. Her eyes watered again and she didn't bother hiding the emotion from her friend. "I should have asked him about the land purchases."

Beth hugged her close. "Sweetie, it's hard to push aside a lifetime of insecurities. I understand that well." She angled back and smiled. "But the risk is so very much worth it."

Megan eyed her friend suspiciously. "You wouldn't happen to know why he bought the wetlands?"

Beth shrugged. "You should be asking him."

"I'm asking you, because I think you know the answer."

"And if I did?" Beth replied enigmatically, "I think it would be wrong for me to tell you. A relationship needs to be built on trust and if I give you the easy answer, then you will have missed an amazing chance to make things right between you."

Beth's words sunk in. Deep. As Megan looked back over her time with Whit, once she'd gotten to know him, he'd been honest, thoughtful, generous. Loving.

The way she'd assumed the worst and walked away had to have hurt him. He had plenty of friends, but no family that had ever come through for him. His father had let him down time and time again.

Even skipping out on bills.

And God, she'd accused Whit of being dishonest. She squeezed her eyes shut and rested her head against the cool steel kennel. At every turn since the tornado, she'd seen his quietly philanthropic spirit. He wasn't the type to shout his good deeds from the rooftops. He didn't seek thanks or accolades.

He was a good man.

And she'd messed up, big-time.

She'd been so afraid of getting hurt, she'd turned her back on the love of a lifetime. As she peeled off her gloves, she made up her mind—she owed Whit an apology. She was done being scared.

In his greenhouse, Whit dug his hands into the dirt and pulled the catnip from its original pot.

The plant had taken off, outgrowing the small container. He'd come out here today to get his thoughts together. About halfway through the night he'd gotten past his pride. Sure, he'd hoped for more trust from Megan. But he'd pushed too much too fast. He needed to back up and regroup.

He wasn't a quitter. He'd worked to build a better life for himself and now he realized how narrow his view of success had been. It wasn't about the house. It was about the people. He just had to figure out the right way to win her back.

He dropped the catnip into a larger container and scooped more potting soil around the exposed roots. He'd made a lot more headway with Megan when he'd given her simpler gifts. But damn it, he'd thought buying the wetlands for her and leaving them untouched was the right decision.

Damn it, he still did. He just needed to find the right time to try again.

The greenhouse door opened and he called out for the deliveryman, "You can leave the crate of plants by the door."

"I don't have any plants to offer." Megan's

voice carried down the long walkway. "Can I stay anyway?"

The sound of her, here, where they'd shared such an amazing night, was like water poured on parched soil. Incredible relief. Hope for new life. But he needed to tread carefully rather than steamrolling her as he'd done too often in the past.

Whit pulled his hands out of the dirt and grabbed a rag. "Did you leave something here last week?"

She walked toward him, every bit as gorgeous in jeans and a T-shirt as she'd been in her lace gown last night. "I did, actually."

Damn, disappointment kicked through him. "What did you leave? I'll keep an eye out for it."

"You already have it in your hands, Whit." She stopped in front of him and pressed her palms to his chest. "I left my heart here with you."

Had he heard her right? "Megan, about last night and the wetlands—"

"Wait." She tapped his lips. "Let me finish. It's important. I brought something for you, but I need to say some things first. I want you to know that I trust you. I know you have an answer and a reason for whatever you've done. We may not agree, but I do respect your right to do as you see fit. We are different, you and I. And that's a good thing too."

"You really mean that."

He was stunned to *his* roots that she gave him her trust so fully. He'd been so used to working like hell for everything in his life. He'd never expected something so perfect, so incredible to land so smoothly in his arms.

"Absolutely." She sounded so sure of herself. Of him. The constant worry in her green eyes was nowhere in sight.

"God, Megan, I l—"

She tapped his mouth again. "I'm still not finished. I need for you to listen. I know I said some unforgivable things last night and I'm sorry. I should have asked for your side of the story rather than assuming."

He held her with his eyes. "I haven't given you a lot of time to trust me. I realize trust has to be earned."

"And you've done that. More times than most

people in this town know and probably far more than I've realized." She stroked his face. "I looked back and realized that you use your money and influence to help so many people without ever taking credit."

He shrugged off those words. "It's easy for me to help. Doesn't put a dent in my bank balance. That's not a sacrifice."

She shook her head. "I think for a kid who was homeless a few times, it probably is a lot tougher to let go of the security of extra money in the bank than you let on."

God, she humbled him and amazed him and made him fall in love with her all over again. "You see me through far nicer eyes than I deserve."

"And you see yourself through a much harsher lens than you should."

Relief shuddered through him as he began to accept that she'd given him a second chance. He wrapped his arms around her waist, hauled her to his chest and just held her, a simple pleasure he would never take for granted again.

He nuzzled her hair, her cinnamon scent tempting his nose and giving him ideas for something new to add to his garden. "What made you change your mind? Who told you about my plans for the wetlands?"

"No one told me about your plans." She angled back to look at him. "I meant it when I said I'm here because I trust you."

"Megan," he said hoarsely. "I bought the tract of land to give to you. It will stay just as it is as a tribute to how damn lucky I am to have you in my life."

Her eyes went misty and then bright with tears. "Are you kidding? Oh my God, Whit." She hugged his neck, kissed him, hugged him again, then dabbed her eyes. "I'm so sorry for doubting you. Can you forgive me?"

"There's nothing to forgive. You're here." He stroked along her back, loving the way she felt in his arms. Loving her, period. "You said you'd brought something for me. What is it?"

"Oh, right." Her tears vanished and she smiled mysteriously. "A couple of things actually for your—our?—house." She reached into her purse and passed him two silver picture frames. The first had a photo taken at the ice rink in Colorado of him with Megan and Evie. The second picture was of Evie on the sofa holding Tallulah, with Truffles, Pixie and Scooter sleeping along the back, while Piper and Cosmo stood by the coffee table set for a tea party.

A lump rose in his throat.

He hauled her close with a ragged sigh. "God, Megan, I love you so damn much. The thought of spending another night wondering if I'd lost you forever…"

"You'll never have to wonder again." She arched up on her toes and brought her lips close to his. "I love you, too, Whit Daltry. Today, tomorrow and forever. Me, you, Evie and our menagerie of animals—we're a family."

"I like the sound of that." A lot. Deciding to leave his heart very much in *her* hands, he knelt on one knee in front of her. "Megan Maguire, will you do me the honor of being my wife, my lover, my love for the rest of our lives? Will you allow me the honor of being a father to Evie and any brothers or sisters we might give her in the years to come? Because there is nothing more that I want than to build a life with you by my side. I love you, Megan. I have a ring too, inside—"

"Yes, yes, with or without a ring, yes." She sank to her knees and took his hands in hers. "Of course, I'll marry you, live with you, love you, for the rest of our lives."

He reached for that quilt he'd never gotten around to putting away and snapped it out onto the floor, then remembered what a mess he was. "We should shower. Together. In the interest of conserving water, you know."

She whispered against his lips. "Oh, we will. But first I have some plans for you and those oranges."

He had some plans for her too. And a lifetime to fulfill them right here in Royal, Texas, where finally he'd put down real roots, thanks to Megan's love.

* * * * *

# MILLS & BOON®

## Why shop at millsandboon.co.uk?

Each year, thousands of romance readers find their perfect read at millsandboon.co.uk. That's because we're passionate about bringing you the very best romantic fiction. Here are some of the advantages of shopping at www.millsandboon.co.uk:

* **Get new books first**—you'll be able to buy your favourite books one month before they hit the shops

* **Get exclusive discounts**—you'll also be able to buy our specially created monthly collections, with up to 50% off the RRP

* **Find your favourite authors**—latest news, interviews and new releases for all your favourite authors and series on our website, plus ideas for what to try next

* **Join in**—once you've bought your favourite books, don't forget to register with us to rate, review and join in the discussions

Visit **www.millsandboon.co.uk**
for all this and more today!